Rachel Watch
Forwar

She had noticed his tall, imposing for ... livestock sale. Dressed in a fringed Western-cut cowhide coat and crisp black felt cowboy hat, he wasn't the only rancher to visit the auction today. Yet he stood out from the others like a rogue stallion, content to stay aloof and alone.

Rugged and rangy, he moved toward her the way a skilled cowboy would move, which heartened her. Rachel resisted the urge to smooth back her hair or fuss with her dress. She was through conforming to the needs and desires of others.

When he introduced himself and lifted his hat, his flint-green eyes remained cold and he didn't smile. "Hello, Rachel. I'm Lincoln Monroe. Are you ready? The sooner we get out of here, the better."

"But we cannot leave yet."

"Why not?"

"I thought Granny Isaacs explained our customs to you during the auction. You and I must be married first."

Dear Reader,

Spring is in the air...and so is romance. Especially at Silhouette, where we're celebrating our 20th anniversary throughout 2000! And Silhouette Desire promises you six powerful, passionate, provocative love stories *every month*.

Fabulous Anne McAllister offers an irresistible MAN OF THE MONTH with *A Cowboy's Secret*. A rugged cowboy fears his darkest secret will separate him from the beauty he loves.

Bestselling author Leanne Banks continues her exciting miniseries LONE STAR FAMILIES: THE LOGANS with a sexy bachelor doctor in *The Doctor Wore Spurs*. In *A Whole Lot of Love*, Justine Davis tells the emotional story of a full-figured woman feeling worthy of love for the first time.

Kathryn Jensen returns to Desire with another wonderful fairy-tale romance, *The Earl Takes a Bride*. THE BABY BANK, a brand-new theme promotion in Desire in which love is found through sperm bank babies, debuts with *The Pregnant Virgin* by Anne Eames. And be sure to enjoy another BRIDAL BID story, which continues with Carol Devine's *Marriage for Sale*, in which the hero "buys" the heroine at auction.

We hope you plan to usher in the spring season with all six of these supersensual romances, only from Silhouette Desire!

Enjoy!

Joan Marlow Golan

Joan Marlow Golan
Senior Editor, Silhouette Desire

Please address questions and book requests to:
Silhouette Reader Service
U.S.: 3010 Walden Ave., P.O. Box 1325, Buffalo, NY 14269
Canadian: P.O. Box 609, Fort Erie, Ont. L2A 5X3

Marriage for Sale
CAROL DEVINE

Published by Silhouette Books
America's Publisher of Contemporary Romance

To Susie

 **SILHOUETTE BOOKS**

ISBN 0-373-76284-4

MARRIAGE FOR SALE

Copyright © 2000 by Carol Devine Rusley

This edition published by arrangement with Harlequin Books S.A.

Visit us at www.romance.net

Printed in U.S.A.

Books by Carol Devine

Silhouette Desire

Beauty and the Beastmaster #816
A Man of the Land #909
The Billionaire's Secret Baby #1218
Marriage for Sale #1284

CAROL DEVINE

lives in Colorado with her husband and three sons, including identical twins. When she's not playing pick-up games of basketball and hunting for lost Reebok footwear, she's holed up in her office, dreaming of romantic heroes.

Her writing has won numerous awards, including the Romance Writers of America's 1992 Golden Heart for Short Contemporary Series Romance. She has also served as president of Rocky Mountain Fiction Writers.

IT'S OUR 20th ANNIVERSARY!
We'll be celebrating all year,
continuing with these fabulous titles,
on sale in March 2000.

Special Edition

#1309 Dylan and the Baby Doctor
Sherryl Woods

#1310 Found: His Perfect Wife
Marie Ferrarella

#1311 Cowboy's Caress
Victoria Pade

#1312 Millionaire's Instant Baby
Allison Leigh

#1313 The Marriage Promise
Sharon De Vita

#1314 Good Morning, Stranger
Laurie Campbell

Intimate Moments

#991 Get Lucky
Suzanne Brockmann

#992 A Ranching Man
Linda Turner

#993 Just a Wedding Away
Monica McLean

#994 Accidental Father
Lauren Nichols

#995 Saving Grace
RaeAnne Thayne

#996 The Long Hot Summer
Wendy Rosnau

Romance

#1432 A Royal Masquerade
Arlene James

#1433 Oh, Babies!
Susan Meier

#1434 Just the Man She Needed
Karen Rose Smith

#1435 The Baby Magnet
Terry Essig

#1436 Callie, Get Your Groom
Julianna Morris

#1437 What the Cowboy Prescribes...
Mary Starleigh

Desire

#1279 A Cowboy's Secret
Anne McAllister

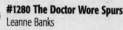

#1280 The Doctor Wore Spurs
Leanne Banks

#1281 A Whole Lot of Love
Justine Davis

#1282 The Earl Takes a Bride
Kathryn Jensen

#1283 The Pregnant Virgin
Anne Eames

#1284 Marriage for Sale
Carol Devine

One

"**N**ext up for bid is Miss Rachel Johnson, as fine a woman as you folks will ever see," bellowed the auctioneer. His resonant voice boomed out over the people milling around the barnyard. Hooking his thumbs under his suspenders, which curved around his ample middle, the auctioneer rocked back on his heels, sweeping the audience with his affable gaze. "At eight and twenty years of age, Miss Rachel is in her prime, and of good, hardworking Johnson stock. Do I hear a bid? The startin' price is one hundred dollars!"

Thinking he must have misheard, Lincoln Monroe checked the rough-hewn wooden platform these people used as an auction block. The sheer volume of sights, sounds and smells made it difficult for him to see and hear what was going on. A sea of buyers and sellers flowed in uneven waves back and forth across the yard, heads covered by calico bonnets and wide-brimmed straw hats. Friends stood gossiping, families strolled holding hands, and children ran laughing and chasing each other. Smells of grilling sausages, roasted corn and fresh-baked pies assaulted Linc's senses, as well. He took his latest purchase, a spirited three-year-old Appaloosa filly, into the wooden corral, shouldered his way past a half dozen horse-drawn wagons and moved closer to the auction block.

Unbelievably, a young woman *was* standing there, dressed in the same old-fashioned gowns as the other women. Caught in at the waist by an unbleached-muslin apron, the long, pale-pink gown buttoned at her neck and brushed the ankles of her black-stockinged legs. Sensible, brown-leather laced boots covered her feet.

Unlike the other women, however, whose heads were covered by bonnets, their hair pinned in neat coils at the back of the neck, this woman had slipped off her bonnet, letting it hang down her back to reveal her near-white, corn silk hair—the straight type that tended to escape its bounds. She had braided hers into many strands and wrapped them like a halo around her head.

She stood up straight on the block, as tall as her short stature allowed, her covered arms hanging loosely at her sides. Wispy blond tendrils accented her heart-shaped face and pointed chin. The honey tint to her complexion, scrubbed free of makeup, was shades darker than the gold of her hair, making her turquoise-colored eyes stand out in startling contrast.

She pursed her lips in serious contemplation as she looked out over the crowd from her high vantage point. She looked nowhere near twenty-eight, but unmistakable composure and maturity kept her chin high and her shoulders thrown back. The ramrod-straight posture pulled her bodice across her breasts—generously rounded breasts that put lust in men's hearts, his included. It made the mystery of why she was being auctioned off like this all the more appalling.

"Come on, folks," called the auctioneer, who tipped his straw hat back on his balding head. "You don't want to hurt Miss Rachel's feelings, do you? When am I going to hear that bid for one hundred dollars? Turn around, honey, and show the folks out there what you have to offer."

The sight of her obediently turning in place chilled Linc. So did the hoots and whistles from the onlookers. Ignoring the catcalls, the woman named Rachel fixed her unblinking turquoise gaze on some faraway point, determined to see her sale through, Linc thought. Her sale into slavery.

Linc wondered which disgusted him more—that a human being was being auctioned off like a piece of meat or that she was actually going along with it. Considering her defiant stance, he'd bet his last world-champion rodeo title that the woman named Rachel didn't have a choice.

Loath as he was to interfere in other people's business, he signaled the auctioneer of his bid in the same way he had all morning, with a tug on the brim of his black Stetson. The bidding didn't pick up much, however, remaining slow, uninterested. Linc wondered about that, too. Even in an insulated environment like this, women like Rachel would be easy to take advantage of, if a man were so inclined.

To his left, a grizzled, gray-bearded man raised his meaty red hand in an obvious bid. A couple of women alongside grinned and elbowed each other, whispering behind their hands. Laughter rippled around them. Linc felt every muscle in his body tense. What was wrong with these people? If he had his hunting rifle, he would have fired into the air and put a stop to this. Poker-faced, he tugged the brim of his Stetson instead.

Up till now, he had cultivated a certain amount of respect for the members of The Community, as they called themselves. Like the Amish or Northern Montana's Hutterites, members of The Community prided themselves on living an old-fashioned and reverential life, dedicated to caring for the land that supported them.

Ever since he'd bought his ranch six months ago, Linc had heard that the best livestock in the region was found at The Community's annual auction, held every spring before planting time. His purchase today of the prize Appy filly and fifty head of mixed-breed cattle proved his sources of information were right. But that didn't explain how supposedly God-fearing people could justify selling one human being to another.

The auctioneer's staccato chant sped up as gray

beard raised his hand again. Linc didn't hesitate in answering. But he did hesitate when a wizened old lady shuffled forward from the crowd and rapped the tall edge of the auction block with her cane, drawing the auctioneer's attention with her high bid, called out in a loud, gravel-edged voice. Linc had assumed all the women were little more than servants to the men.

The forcefulness of the old lady's manner surprised him, too, especially when he bid again. She spun around and wagged the knobby-headed cane in his face. "You are an outsider, sir," she hissed. "I'd advise you to stay out of our business."

Linc didn't bother to give her the courtesy of tipping his hat, and he exaggerated his West Texas drawl into sarcasm. "Well, howdy-do to you, ma'am. I may be an outsider here, but I pretty much do what I damn well please whether it's my business or not."

"And what I'm saying to you, young man," she retorted, peering at him through crescents of wrinkles, "is that you don't have the faintest idea what you are getting yourself into. All I can say is, I hope you're a bachelor."

"A bachelor? What for? So when you have me drawn and quartered for interfering in your so-called business, I won't be leaving a widow?"

She snorted and thrust the cane at the middle of his chest, ruffling the leather fringe of his buff suede cattleman's jacket. "Don't say I didn't warn you."

Linc ignored her and raised his next bid considerably, proving his contempt. Clearly unimpressed, the old lady rapped the auction block again, upping her bid.

Linc tugged his hat brim again. "You're going to lose. I don't care what I have to pay."

"Our laws regarding women of Rachel's age are very specific," she informed him while keeping the bidding alive. "You'd do well to heed my words. We take care of our own."

Linc spoke through gritted teeth. "Is this how you take care of your own? Selling a defenseless young woman? No way can you justify this."

She waved her cane at him in dismissal. "Yet you are bidding for her. You are participating in what you call unjustifiable."

"I'm buying her for one reason and one reason only—to give the lady her freedom."

"Freedom, hmm?" Her wrinkled-raisin eyes brightened in renewed consideration. "Perhaps you are not as high and mighty as you appear."

Linc iced her with one glare. "Don't count on it."

"You are angry. That is good. Rachel knows how to handle anger and the single-mindedness of a beast obsessed. Instead of freeing her, perhaps you should consider keeping her for your own use."

"My own use? What kind of people are you?"

"Simple people. That is our motto. We began as a collection of dreamers and doers, and became The Community. It is the way we choose to live."

Linc stabbed his finger toward the auction block. "Does Rachel have a choice?"

"Of course she does. She asked to be sold in this manner. It is her right."

"Then she must be even more brainwashed than you are."

The old lady cackled with glee. "You speak your mind as does she. I have reconsidered. The two of you will be well matched."

Linc shook his head in disgust at the crazy ramblings of the old woman and, determined to bring an end to this charade, signaled a huge jump in the size of his bid. The auctioneer incorporated the amount in his chant, and the audience gasped.

"Going, going, gone!" the auctioneer announced, pointing at Linc. "Sold to the clean-shaven outsider in the black cowboy hat."

It sickened Linc to breathe the same air as these people as he pushed his way to the auctioneer. The women in their bonnets and the men in their straw hats parted before him in apparent awe.

Linc didn't understand them. He didn't want to understand them. All he wanted to do was pay his money and get the woman named Rachel out of here.

Rachel watched her buyer come forward to claim her.

She had noticed his tall, imposing form previously during the livestock sale. Dressed in a fringed, Western-cut cowhide coat and crisp black felt cowboy hat, he wasn't the only rancher to visit the auction this day. Yet he stood out from the others like a rogue stallion, content to stay aloof and alone. He ignored the tables of farm produce and canned goods and the friendly overtures of the sellers who made them.

Rugged and rangy, he moved toward her with economy, the way a skilled cowboy would move, which heartened her. Appreciation of the vast land

and its creatures was an important attribute in a man. If the cattle he'd bought this morning were any indication, he had a good eye for quality. His worn-denim jeans and silver belt buckle also spoke of an experienced cattleman. Trim and fit, he carried himself with the authority of a substantial landowner. Another point in his favor was the three-year-old Appaloosa filly he'd bought earlier—the finest prospective cutting horse in the lot.

Rachel resisted the urge to smooth back her hair or fuss with her dress. She was through making herself conform to the needs and desires of others. Either he accepted her as she was or she would find another path to the life she was determined to set for herself.

Her buyer shook hands with the auctioneer, and Rachel examined his lean-jawed face. Harsh prairie sun and wind had burnished his skin and etched squint lines around his eyes. Thick lashes and thicker brows were as black as his hat. His straight nose matched the uncompromising lines of his mouth while day-old whiskers shadowed his cheeks. He seemed a fine specimen of a man.

But when he introduced himself and lifted his hat to her, his flint-green eyes remained cold and he didn't smile. "Hello, Rachel. I'm Lincoln Monroe."

He had the kind of low and dusty voice that led people to listen closely. Tremors traveled up her arm as she pumped his swallowing hand. "Pleased to meet you, Lincoln Monroe."

"Linc is fine."

"Linc." Accustomed to the biblical names the people of The Community favored, his name felt foreign on her tongue. The tremors she felt were also foreign to her and traversed across and down her body, flushing it with unfamiliar warmth. She tried not to show it, acting natural as could be, but he must have sensed the power of her feeling, for his jaw tightened and he questioned her with his gaze.

She did not move. He possessed the penetrating gaze of a hunter—ever hungry and ever searching. The direct force of it pinned her in place as surely as if she were his prey.

Confusion hit her—she refused to be prey for anyone or anything. Yet the danger she felt emanating from him exhilarated her. Instinct told her he was different from everyone else, that he was worthy of trust. In spite of the fact that she was a stranger to him, he had bid for her, confirming the fact that she truly wasn't as strange and ugly as so many claimed.

She met his gaze for a long, wordless moment before he broke it off, his jaw set more tightly than ever.

Attuned to his changing mood, Rachel straightened her backbone and watched him turn to the cashier as the people surrounding them witnessed in hushed silence. She wasn't surprised by their reaction. No other member of The Community, man or woman, had ever been sold for such a high price.

She expected Lincoln Monroe to examine her before paying his money, as was his right, but he didn't ask her to read anything or test the strength of her arms. Instead he pulled out his wallet and paid in one-hundred-dollar bills. That might be a problem, breaking those bills into lesser currency, she thought.

"Follow me," he said curtly, cutting his way

through the throng. She barely had time to accept her selling price from the cashier and pocket the roll of money in her skirt.

He should have ordered her to walk before him, so all in The Community could see, at last, that she was worth coveting. But he was unfamiliar with her customs and striding fast, as well, and because her legs didn't match the long length of his, she had to trot to keep up. Some folks snickered, but she kept her gaze focused straight ahead and concentrated on the comforting solidity of her buyer's broad back.

The denim he wore fitted his legs with little material to spare, hiding his cowboy boots down to the well-worn heels. His cowboy hat offset the thick coal-black hair at his nape. The length was trimmed neatly compared to most men she knew but Rachel decided that his matched the angular lines of his body and no-nonsense strides. The trim of his forelock in front had done little to soften the rather grim expression he had greeted her with, but she no longer cared about that. She knew how to gentle any soul, human or otherwise.

Just thinking about her future with him made her heart beat like a tiny bird's. She had learned long ago that a person's appearance wasn't nearly as important as the content of their character. But when it came right down to lying together and the business of making babies, she couldn't imagine how it might be done if the man and the woman didn't see some sort of beauty in each other.

He halted at his rig, and Rachel had a moment to examine the large black truck, taking in the fat wheels and metal frame. It was the outsider's version of a wagon, made for hauling heavy loads, only it roared like a bear and spewed noxious-smelling smoke. Rachel told herself to prepare to get inside it. The marriage ceremony would only take a few minutes. Then she would be his and he, hers.

She was glad to see that the horse trailer behind the truck was clean and in good repair. The filly, raised free on The Community's pastures, deserved fine quarters and the best of care. Fortunately the truck was parked close to her corral. She already had plenty of opportunity to familiarize herself with such a modern contraption.

"Where's your stuff?" Linc asked.

Rachel broke from her reverie. "Stuff?"

"Bags, luggage—whatever it is you want to take with you," he replied.

"My trunk contains most of my possessions." She pointed to a large trunk close by. "The rest I will fetch myself."

She literally ran off. Linc examined the trunk. Bright brass rivets stretched the leather over the wooden frame. New leather, not dyed. It hadn't had a chance to age like the one that had been passed down to him from his great-grandmother. But in every other way it was identical.

Rachel returned, lugging her saddle with both arms in front of her, with her most precious possessions tucked into the parfleche slung over one shoulder. Linc got one look at her and wrested the saddle from her. "This is way too heavy for you to carry."

"I've been carrying it for most of my life," she

replied, her tone milder and more pliant than she intended. She had heard rumors about how outsiders often took their women for granted. He must not feel he had dominion over her.

Linc threw the saddle alongside her trunk in the bed of his truck. "You've been treated like a beast of burden. That's not going to happen anymore."

"Hard work soothes my soul."

"Yeah? Is that why you agreed to be auctioned off like a piece of meat?"

"My last relation died last year." She shrugged. "Obviously, I could not live alone."

"Obviously." Although he had been called a male chauvinist more than once in his life, even he understood the misogyny implied in her statement. It was one more strike against this supposed utopia, The Community. "Let's go," he said in a clipped voice. "The sooner we get out of here, the better."

"I thought Granny Isaacs explained our customs to you during the auction. You and I must be married first."

"Excuse me?"

"An unmarried man and an unmarried woman of similar age are not allowed to live together."

He took her arm, hurrying her toward the truck. "Don't worry. We won't be living together."

"But—"

The old lady who had given him such a hard time separated from the watchdog crowd and pushed her way between them. She stabbed a gnarled finger at the middle of Linc's chest. "Are we of The Community, who have had Rachel with us for her whole life, supposed to take you at your word?'' she demanded.

"You of all people know what my intentions are," Linc retorted.

"Do I? You are little more than a stranger to us."

"Please, Linc," interrupted Rachel. "Granny Isaacs is right. Unless we are wed, you will not be allowed to take me with you. It is for my protection should I be ill-treated."

"You have got to be kidding." Tempted to just pack her into the cab of his truck, Linc realized that strong-arming her was precisely why these people were insisting on the commitment that marriage implied. "What if I'm already involved with someone else?" His casual relationships with various women didn't exactly qualify, but he wasn't about to back down. Not when *his* freedom was at stake.

"Rachel will be sold to another."

Linc appealed to Rachel. "Look, you and I are on the same side here. I wouldn't have spent my money if I wasn't going to take good care of you."

"Money is not enough of a guarantee," interrupted Granny Isaac.

"I can't believe this," he said. "If the granny's bid had won over mine, you wouldn't have to marry her."

"The commitment The Community requires is the same," Rachel explained. "Both parties must pledge to treat each other with respect."

Granny Isaacs chimed in. "Certainly we can require no less from you."

Linc wheeled on her. "Yes, you can. You have my word."

"We require more than your word," she replied. "We require you and Rachel to be legally wed."

"How in hell can this be legal? There's no blood test, no waiting period."

"The federal laws of this country waive such requirements when they violate certain religious practices."

"You can't force me to get married," Linc said. The no-promises, no-demands, confirmed-bachelor part of him wanted to throw his hands up and leave the place. But he refused to walk away, not when a human being's freedom was at stake.

"There is nothing forced about this marriage," Granny Isaacs informed him. "Rachel gave her consent when she agreed to be sold at the auction. You, on the other hand, are free to refuse."

Their little discussion was drawing quite a crowd. Linc folded his arms over his chest in disgust. "What's to stop me from going through with this idiotic marriage bit, then annulling the thing the minute we hit the nearest town?"

"An annulment requires both your consent. If it is granted, there is nothing I can do to prevent it."

The noise of a sharply rude whistle ripped through the air. "Rachel Johnson!" yelled a woman, her face sneering. "He doesn't want you, after all."

"Give 'im back his money!" another woman screamed.

Linc grabbed Rachel's hand and tugged her toward

the truck. "I'm taking you away from this crazy place."

Rachel twisted from his grasp. "I won't go unless we are married. Please, Linc. It is our law." Desperation shadowed those extraordinary eyes.

He pulled her aside, out of earshot of the others.

"If I have to marry you to get you out of here, then we'll do it. But I want an annulment as soon as we hit town."

Faced by his clear reluctance, Rachel shook her head. "It is unfair to hold you to traditions that were unknown to you at the time of the auction."

"That isn't what I asked you. Do you want to marry me or not?"

Rachel didn't have to check the curious expressions of those witnessing to know that she, too, wished to understand what made him bid for her in the first place. That was what she wanted. "Of course I want to marry you."

"Good." To shut up the rude naysayers, he sealed the bargain with a sudden kiss.

Surprise dropped Rachel's mouth. Amused, he brushed the hair off her forehead and flashed his first smile, brilliant white in the sun. "Everybody is watching us, but I don't think they're convinced of my sincerity. Why don't we give them a show?"

He then kissed her with far more intent. He shaped her mouth, parting her lips, causing tingles to shoot down her legs. Caught off-balance, she clutched at his arms. The tip of his tongue teased her and all sense of equilibrium fled. Wrapping her arms around his neck, she clung to him.

He ended the kiss abruptly, searching her expression. The wariness in his gaze made her instinctively hold her breath, and she wondered what he might do next. Hunger underscored his wariness, hunger far sharper and raw than what she had witnessed earlier. And she had aroused it, Rachel realized.

The arousal went both ways. The heady yearning she felt must have been transparent, for his wariness flared into warning. "The deal is," he said softly so only she could hear him, "marriage, then annulment. Don't expect anything more."

He faced the murmuring onlookers, giving her no time to argue. But she wouldn't argue in front of these people. She'd been singled out and ridiculed at one time or another by most of them, and she had no intention of giving anyone reason to talk about her now.

As a young child, it was her supposedly albino hair they commented on. Positively ghostly, they'd said. When her parents replied that she was simply light blond, the focus shifted to the uncanny color of her eyes. Even her father declared them unreal. Once she started school, she didn't know how to defend herself when other kids called her "spooky" for seeming to look right through them.

Contributing to the problem was her habit of staring out the windows, daydreaming. Many times she was forced to sit in front of the class with horse blinders on, big black square ones that kept her focused straight ahead. She supposed the punishment was intended to teach her a lesson. It simply gave the other children more reason to call her names.

After she'd grown up and left school, she learned

to forget her old hurts by roaming the range lands for hours at a time. When questioned by her parents about what she was doing out there, she described a band of wild horses roaming the hills. Her plan to tame some of those horses and sell them at auction did not go over well. To her family, it was an impossible task because her help was needed at home on the farm. Even the few friends she'd managed to make said she needed to improve her dismaying lack of cooking skills and learn a trade rather than waste her time running around the countryside. After all, as an adult member of The Community, she was expected to do her share of the work.

But Rachel believed deep in her heart that she was doing her share. Horses had a language all their own, a language she had learned to speak. Surely that was more valuable than anything else she could possibly do.

Her claim to be able to speak to horses turned out to be the biggest mistake she'd ever made. Even Granny Isaacs took her aside and told Rachel she was far too old for such fantasies.

Admittedly, "speak" may not have been the best word to use when describing what she did. Listening to horses would have been more accurate. But in the end, she definitely got the message. No one wanted to listen to her. And Linc was proving to be no exception.

He packed her under his arm and looked over their audience. "Make no mistake about it. I wanted Rachel from the moment I saw her," he announced. "You want me to prove it by seeing us married? Then do it now or forever hold your peace."

Two

"**G**ranny Isaacs," Rachel said, taking solace in the wise old eyes of her mentor, who didn't seem perturbed at all by Linc's intimidation. "Will you perform the ceremony?"

"Of course." With her cane she pointed to a nearby grassy area and Rachel obeyed by leading Linc there.

"Don't tell me she's a minister, too?" He snorted.

"The eldest of the elders. The elders advise and minister to us. Do you object to my choice?"

"Just get on with it."

Granny Isaacs nodded in agreement. "Indeed we shall. Stand side by side, please, and hold each other's hands."

Rachel ignored the head shaking of her neighbors

and other members of The Community. They'd had much the same reaction when she announced her intention to be sold at the auction. She had heard more than one whisper that she was likely to draw the lowest price ever recorded, that the reason no one wanted to take her in was because of her peculiar opinions and strange ways. Few in The Community were willing to buck the collective wisdom of the many.

Granny Isaacs clasped their hands together with her cool veined and gnarled fingers. "The bonding of man and woman is a sacred event," she began. "Do both of you understand the meaning of this?"

"Yes," Rachel said.

"Yes," Linc echoed, mystified by the unorthodox start to the ceremony. But then, everything these people did was unorthodox.

Linc pushed the incongruous smell of new clover, sight of the clapboard barn and whispers of the onlookers from his mind. The age-old words of the traditional ceremony, however, spoken in Granny Isaacs grave and gravelly voice, weighed on his conscience. He figured if she wasn't worried about the fact that he was lying through his teeth, he shouldn't be. But Rachel recited her vows with equal gravity, her blue gaze locked with his, and the resentment he felt at being put in this position pushed him into rushing through his vows without regard to anybody's feelings save his own.

He waved at Granny Isaacs to skip over the exchange of rings. "No, wait," Rachel said.

She reached under the collar of her gown and withdrew a braided chain necklace, anchored by two rings.

They clinked as she slipped them off the chain, and she offered Linc the smaller of the two. "These wedding bands belonged to my late parents. I'd like you to use my mother's ring as my wedding band."

Plain gold, the ring was scratched in many places. Linc sensed it had been worn for a very long time by hands that had done a great deal of work. Still warm from her body heat, the ring clearly had enormous sentimental value to Rachel. He felt awkward taking it. The fact that the bride was providing her own wedding ring proved how surreal this whole situation was.

Rachel held out her hand with graceful expectancy. Slipping the ring onto her finger was an exercise in self will. Linc tried to shake the feeling that her mother must be spinning in her grave.

He realized his choice of ring fingers was incorrect when it was Rachel's turn. She slipped her father's ring onto the third finger of his left hand. Her smile reassured him that the mistake didn't matter. Linc didn't care to be reassured. What difference did it make if he put the ring on her second finger or her third?

The minute Granny Isaacs pronounced them husband and wife, he said, "Come on, Rachel. We're leaving."

He stalked through the gathering who'd witnessed the ceremony, towing Rachel by the hand. She had to have the coldest hands in the history of the universe. Her fingers wove their way between his until their hands were clasped palm to palm. He allowed it, but it annoyed him, as though she were taking advantage of his good graces.

Approaching the truck, she pointed out his new filly.

"You are a fine judge of horseflesh," she said.

It was a compliment, but acknowledging it felt like a concession to him. Maybe it was her use of the word horseflesh. "Thanks," he said gruffly.

"What shall we name her?" she asked.

"Not we. I own her. I'll name her," he said, more annoyed than ever.

"She's got the fire of the sun in her chestnut coat and a blinding white blanket. If she were mine, I would name her Summer."

"What kind of name is that?"

She frowned, obviously bothered by the tone of judgment in his voice. "A perfect name."

"Fine. Her name is Summer." It really didn't matter what the horse was called. She would be sold at a very nice profit once she was fully trained. Linc slapped on a pair of leather roping gloves. "Get in the truck while I load her."

"I will help."

She wasn't asking—she was telling. His annoyance increased tenfold. Who did she think she was? "Wait in the damned pickup," he ordered.

"Please do not swear at me, Linc. I may be of help. I know horses."

"I know horses, too. Get in the truck, *Mrs.* Monroe."

Rachel put her hands on her hips, but surpressed her frustration. She didn't wish to create another scene, not minutes after their wedding ceremony.

Tapping her foot, she stayed beside the truck, ready to help at a moment's notice.

She hadn't realized it before, but the trailer was positioned with its loading door flush against the corral. Linc removed the fence posts that blocked the door, then opened it and pulled down the ramp. It thudded on the damp ground.

Summer stood at the other end of the corral, ears pricked forward in curiosity, her dark tail swishing at the flies buzzing around her bay coat and spotted white Appaloosa blanket. She wasn't quite sure what to make of the noise and activity caused by the man in the black cowboy hat but, so far, she wasn't unduly alarmed, Rachel noticed.

Linc paid little attention to Summer at this stage, keeping his eyes averted while preparing the trailer. He tied a rope to the trailer door, which mystified Rachel, but she approved of the generous fork load of hay he tossed in the trailer. By this time of day, Summer would be hungry.

Walking toward the horse, he spoke soothingly. Rachel couldn't hear the words but soothing or not, Summer took off in a typical fast-paced lope. She balked at the unfamiliar sight of the trailer ramp, but, behind her, Linc waved his hat and his arms. Frightened, Summer had two choices—run over the man or escape into the trailer. She escaped into the trailer. Linc used the rope to slam shut the door before the horse could back out, avoiding any possibility that he might get kicked. A moment later, the ramp was stowed and he was rounding the truck, dusting his hands.

"Why did you scare her so?" Rachel demanded.

"It worked, didn't it? I want to get out of here."
He opened the passenger door for her and trotted to
the other side. Settling in, he gunned the engine and
checked the rear view mirror, thankful he caught a
break in loading the filly—Summer—fairly easily.
Now if he could just get her home without a
hitch...that is, if Rachel cooperated. She was still
standing next to the truck, waiting to give him more
grief, no doubt. "Rachel, for the last time, get in or
I swear, I'll leave you behind."

She ducked her head, puzzlement on her face.
"How do I get in?"

"You're kidding me, right?"

"No, I don't believe so."

"Don't tell me you haven't been in a truck before?"

"I'm afraid not."

"Twenty-eight years old and you've never learned
to drive?"

"I've been driving teams since I was a youngster,"
she offered.

"I take it you mean you've been driving teams of
horses," he commented dryly.

"Four in hand and eight in hand. Among those in
The Community, I am considered quite good."

"I bet." He showed her how to work the handle
of the door, then opened it for her. She reached for
his arm and gathered her skirt. He boosted her inside
the truck, all too aware of his bird's-eye view of her
well-shaped rump. The long dress followed her moves

gracefully, including the awkward hiking up she had to do to sit in her seat.

Settling the skirt around her legs, she turned her bright, white smile on him. "Thank you."

He nodded, rather than reply, refusing to give away the lust he felt. Never been kissed, never been married—what was *wrong* with the men around here?

Plunking down behind the steering wheel, he checked the rearview mirror, hoping the filly had settled down. No, not the filly. "Summer." Linc rolled his eyes. "We'll be heading into the town of Tall Timber first."

"I expected as much." Rachel noticed the sure way he handled the steering of the truck. The confusing mix of levers and dials and displays that made up the dashboard unnerved her. The engine roared into life, startling her enough to cause Linc to comment.

"There is nothing to be scared of."

"Good." Still she wondered what she had gotten herself into. The answer came in the square male knees and taut thighs encased in blue denim edging her vision. Lean muscle bunched as he pumped the pedals built into the floor of the truck. In the enclosed cab, the back of his hands loomed large and dark. She had just held those hands and been comforted by their strength. But the look of that strength now raised gooseflesh along her arms. He'd better be gentle with her, she thought. He was so much bigger than she.

She jumped as his arm snaked behind her neck along the top of her seat. He twisted to look out the rear window, oblivious, it seemed, to her total awareness of him. He backed the truck out slow and easy and started down the rutted dirt road that would take them directly to the highway. "I was wondering if you might be intimidated about going to town."

"It is thoughtful of you to mention it. I must admit I am. Most people in my situation would be."

"There is nothing to worry about. Tall Timber is a nice little town. You'll get used to living there in no time."

"Am I mistaken?" she asked. "I thought you owned a ranch."

"I do. It's very isolated, though. Believe me, you'll be better off in Tall Timber. You can make friends and have a regular life."

"I beg to differ. I am not one for friends, for gossip and socializing." She removed the roll of money from her skirt and showed it to him. "What I had hoped to do was to turn some of my bought price into smaller bills."

"They gave you the money I paid for you?"

"It is my stake for the future. I wish to use a small portion for clothes similar to the denim you wear, for working on your ranch."

"Did you really think I bought you to have you slave around my ranch?"

Her confused expression told Linc that was exactly what she thought. "Let me make myself clear," he said. "I bought you to free you."

"Free me from what?"

"Bondage. I want you to be able to live your own life, without other people telling you what to do. You should be on your own, discovering what is important to you."

"I already know what is important to me. You."

Linc swore under his breath. "That's what I mean. You shouldn't build your life around anybody, especially a man. Your life belongs to you."

"My life does belong to me in the way that you say. But now I dedicate myself to spending my life with you."

"I free you from your obligation. Y'see, I'm not interested. The only reason I bought you was to prevent you from being sold to somebody else."

"I am a good worker, a good companion. I promise to be of much value to you on your ranch. That is the life I most enjoy, the life I know best."

"Don't you ever dream of seeing more than a Podunk community in the middle of Montana?"

"Montana is my home. Why would I wish to leave the place where I have found my most profound happiness?"

It was hard to argue with profound happiness. It was also hard to argue with an unsophisticated thinker like Rachel. "Trust me on this, honey. Give Tall Timber a chance. You won't have to answer to anybody. I'll walk you through finding a job and a place to live. Then you'll have a chance to be on your own."

"You are to leave me alone there?" She sounded shocked and looked it, too, with her eyes widening, making him think of storm clouds moving across a brilliant blue sky.

"Tall Timber is not a big city or anything. Believe me, it won't be as hard as you think."

"This is not right. Husbands and wives are supposed to stay together. This is not what I agreed to, when I said my wedding vows."

"You're not exactly in a position to refuse."

"Of course I may refuse. I will not allow myself to be abused in this way."

"Abused! I'm trying to help you, for God's sake."

"For God's sake? I think not. You aren't interested in my welfare. You said my happiness is of so little consequence that I should give it up in favor of living among strangers. I return to you my selling price. Please take me back to The Community so I may be sold to someone else."

"Put your money away, Rachel. You're not going back."

"Then take me to your ranch."

He inwardly counted to ten, all patience gone. He didn't care how new to the modern world she was; he wasn't taking her to his ranch. "We'll take a drive through Tall Timber. You'll see what a nice town it is. Who knows, you may change your mind."

"I never change my mind."

He sent her a sharp glance. "There isn't a woman alive who doesn't."

"Then you have never met a woman like me."

He gave her a good once-over, but she was staring out the window, ignoring him, which made him all the more impatient with her. What was her problem? She had to recognize the fact that living in town was going to be plenty easier than living with a wild good-ol' boy on a windswept ranch in the middle of no-where.

If he was going to change her mind, he needed to

give her his full and undivided attention. The kind of attention she might not particularly like, but it would definitely change her mind. Without warning, he pulled the truck over to the side of the road.

"Why are you stopping?"

The tiniest bit of alarm flickered in her eyes. Finally, he thought. "Why do you think you can trust me—a man you know nothing about?"

"You are my husband. I trust you because of it."

"You just met me. Maybe I bought you for the worst of reasons."

Her expression softened, blossoming into one of complete understanding. "Linc, if you were a man of unsavory character, you would not have bothered to purchase me, a complete stranger to you."

Such unshakable conviction was going to land her in plenty of hot water if she wasn't careful. "Maybe I'm not as noble as you think."

He wound strong fingers around her wrist and guided the tips of her fingers to his mouth. Baring his teeth, he let the edges caress each fingertip. Only it wasn't a caress. Her whole body stiffened at the flood of sensation. Every pore seemed to ignite, licking her skin like candle flame, leaving moisture in its wake in the same way his teeth left moisture, and his tongue. The tip tickled the pads of her fingers and slid between them, the heat of him equal to the heat breaking out on her brow.

Her heart heated, too, pounding like a hammer on an anvil, singing in her ears. Breathing became impossible, much less speaking. Besides, what was there to say? Every fiber of her being felt fired from within.

She scarcely knew what to do, where to look. In spite of the fact that she was seated, support fled her limbs. Most shocking of all was the urge to bring his fingers to her lips and bare her teeth to him as well.

Loath to show her complete ignorance as to how to respond to him, she licked dry lips. The forest color of his eyes, so near, pooled with sudden obsidian.

All breath fled from her then. Suspended by the oddest sense of anticipation, her whole body shivered in awareness of him. And he of her, she instinctively sensed.

His grip on her wrist diminished as his thumb stroked the inner skin. His muscles coiled like her own, readying for what, she didn't know. But she wanted to find out. Oh, how she wanted to find out.

The sharp bang of hooves hit metal. Rachel jumped, but it was Linc who understood what was happening. He shot from the truck before Rachel could get her limp legs moving.

"Summer!" she gasped.

By the time she levered the door open and leaped to the ground, Linc had slid open the trailer's paneled window and peered inside. "Damn horse."

"Is she all right?"

"She's restless as hell. We better get moving. I don't want to take a chance on her injuring herself." Without wasting a moment, Linc grasped Rachel by the elbow and hoisted her into the truck. "You're going to get your wish, little lady. To the ranch we go. I don't have time to fool around with you and the filly, too."

Was that what he was doing? Making a fool of her? she wondered.

Linc was gratified to have finally hit on a strategy that left her speechless, and he filed the information away for future use. He wasn't sure what was going on in that incomprehensible mind of hers, but he aimed to do whatever was necessary to ensure her prompt departure from his life.

He certainly wasn't going to let her stay at his ranch. It was a good thing, too. He had no intention of letting this woman get close to him. Normally he didn't go for the naive type. Rachel, however, presented an interesting combination of traits. Twenty-eight-year-old virgins didn't grow on trees, especially virgins with her head-turning looks. In fact, he might have questioned the virginity claim—until he had kissed her. Rachel didn't know how to kiss. She didn't know how to hide that fact, either, despite her apparent determination to hold onto her poise and ignore the slings and arrows of a bunch of narrow-minded hicks.

Rachel still blushed for heaven's sake. Her eyes still widened in sensual awareness. Linc felt his own eyes narrow at the prospect of helping her discover where such awareness could lead. He was, after all, a normal, red-blooded American male. Those shallow, excited pants she took when he had kissed her damn near burst the buttons on his jeans.

A stolen moment or two was the only satisfaction he was going to get from this deal, however, and he knew it. The confinement of committed relationships didn't appeal to him in the least. It was bad enough he had to go through with the charade of a wedding ceremony to get her out of The Community.

Unfortunately, he was getting the feeling that she was taking the marriage bit way too seriously. His work was cut out for him. Even though he had taken great pains before the wedding ceremony to explain his intentions—or lack thereof—he was unsure if Rachel understood how little the wedding vows meant to him. The whole idea of staying committed to one person for an entire lifetime didn't make sense. Human beings just weren't built that way. His wild and wooly days on the rodeo circuit proved it—or more accurately, his wild and wooly nights. Harsh experience told him that most women were no more inclined toward fidelity than he was, a lesson he'd learned the hard way.

To spare Rachel the same lesson, he would give her some hints about his true nature. After all, she needed to learn how to handle herself with guys like him before he sent her out in the cold, cruel world.

"How many times have you been to Tall Timber?" he asked.

"None."

"None?"

"None," she reiterated, still smarting from the disconcerting thought that Linc was merely fooling around with her.

"Have you been to any other towns?"

"No."

"Cities?"

She sensed his searching glance and shook her head.

"What about the other members of The Community?"

"Other than health emergencies where specialized doctors are required, traveling outside The Community is simply not done."

"Don't people need to buy tools and other farming equipment?"

"Tools and other implements are forged by blacksmiths. What can't be made is delivered."

"What about food, groceries?"

"We grow our own food."

"All of it?"

"What we can't grow we trade for at the Hudson Valley co-op with our canned goods." Somewhat mollified by his interest, Rachel relented, expanding her answer. "Our pickled peppers and mint-flavored peaches are in much demand."

"You can't preserve all your food. What about refrigeration?"

"The refrigeration you are referring to requires electric power. The use of such power is discouraged in order to maintain the connection to the land and the values of simplicity that go with it. However, I am familiar with gas heat. The elders encourage its use in our homes because the winters in Montana are so long and cold."

"Isn't that against the so-called rules?"

"We have adopted some modern conveniences to protect from the worst of winter weather. The safekeeping of the oldest and youngest is of primary importance in all families, wouldn't you agree?"

"Does that mean you have indoor plumbing?"

"Each farmhouse has an individual pipe which delivers clean water."

"So old Granny Isaacs has to trot to the outhouse in the middle of winter to take care of business. Is that what you're saying?"

"The outhouse is out-of-doors for good reason. Would you have it any other way?"

He blew out a great gust of air and tipped his hat back on his head in disbelief. "How old are you again?"

"Eight and twenty."

"Next time say twenty-eight. Can you at least read?"

"Certainly."

"You went to school?"

"The Community takes the education of its children very seriously. Of course I went to school."

"How long?"

"Through the eighth grade."

"Through the eighth grade," he repeated, damning the place where she came from once again in his mind. Clearly, she was going to have to learn a lot more about the outside world. She wouldn't make it on her own otherwise. And right now he didn't see any alternative but to become her teacher. "For the time being, leaving you in town by yourself may not be the best idea I've ever had. You need to learn how to cope first."

"Learning how to cope with you will be a useful skill indeed."

He examined her, his green eyes narrow. "Believe me, I'll teach you everything you need to know."

Rachel quailed at the thought. Yet also felt exhilarated. Afraid that he might be making fun of her again, Rachel held his gaze. ''What do you mean?'' she asked pointedly.

''For one thing, get used to the idea that you'll be moving to town at some point. I figure it may take you a week or two to learn how to cope. If you don't cooperate—''

''You are my husband,'' Rachel replied stiffly. ''Of course I shall cooperate.''

''Is that what you've been doing for the past hour—cooperating?''

''I have an unfortunate habit of speaking my mind. Forgive me.''

''I want you to speak your mind,'' he said, in what sounded to her like exaggerated forbearance. ''But you better be listening when I'm speaking about what's on my mind. Specifically, learning what I want you to learn.''

She placed her hand over her heart in a grand show of her own forbearance. ''I swear on my mother's grave. Or do you wish for me to cross my heart and hope to die?'' she asked tartly.

What he wished was for her to stop using those quaint expressions he remembered using as a kid—when he was still playful and innocent. ''No,'' he retorted. ''I want you alive so I can wring your scrawny little neck.''

Rachel clapped her hand over her mouth to keep from smiling too broadly at him. It was one thing to bait a bear—quite another to provoke him. She had made her point. Rubbing it in would accomplish nothing. Removing her hand, she wagged her finger at him. "You are a great one for joshing."

"The word is joking," he said, sending her the sternest of glances. "Use it."

"Joking," she repeated obediently, though she was having trouble maintaining a reasonably sober expression.

"That's your first lesson. The next one is to realize that Tall Timber is going to be your future home. I'll give you until the end of the month to get ready to live there. After that, you'll be on your own whether you're ready or not."

"I understand. However, you shall not regret your decision to take me to your ranch. Thank you."

"I'm already regretting it, thanks to you," he groused.

Rachel hid her smile so as not to antagonize him further. Horses, her most favorite of animals, had their own way of grousing, too. They liked to put up a spirited resistance when asked to comply with her wishes. It was their way of reminding her that they weighed far more than she did and possessed lethal power. But her willingness to speak until she was fully heard kept the balance of power intact.

There was little doubt in her mind that though Linc was less than enthusiastic about their marriage, once he understood what a valuable asset she was on his ranch, he wouldn't want to let her go—either as a help mate or a wife.

Three

———

"**G**ood gracious, Linc, what a marvel to behold. Your ranch is beyond anything I could have imagined," Rachel exclaimed when the pickup crested the last hill, revealing the panoramic view that included the main buildings of the Triple M Ranch. Designed to look as though it had sprung from this land more than a century ago, the buildings blended into the austere landscape, with their weathered barn siding and steep, shake roofs.

"Don't get any ideas," he warned, dedicated to squelching her enthusiasm. "You won't be staying here long."

"Even so, I've rarely seen such a sight. And look at your dogs. I love dogs." In one quick move, she hopped from the pickup before it came to a complete stop and waded into the yapping pack, showing a complete and utter disregard for her own safety.

"Rachel!" By the time he halted the truck, the dogs were swarming around her like bees to honey. Luckily they were friendly, but Rachel couldn't have known that when she took it into her head to jump from a moving truck. She needed more than a few lessons on how to survive in town. She needed to be taught how to survive, period.

Shaking his head in disbelief, Linc opened the gate to the nearest round pen and drove the entire rig inside. Once he let down the trailer door in back, Summer would come charging out. Shortcuts like spooking a horse into submission always resulted in more work down the line, especially with a spirited, inexperienced filly like this one. But in this case, he had little choice.

His ranch foreman, Bud Sylvester, an athletically trim, grizzled cattle veteran, showed up in the yard to see what the ruckus was all about. Following from the bunkhouse, came the motherly form of Linda Amato, the ranch housekeeper, wearing her customary double pocket smock, gingham blouse, blue jeans and red banana. Rachel ran toward them with the barking pack of dogs at her heels, her skirt flying, gaily waving hello like she'd known them all her life.

Linc could only imagine what Bud and Linda must be thinking at the sight of Rachel. Her long dress alone marked her as a member of The Community. Even if they were as ignorant as he had been about their customs and didn't guess about the marriage, he still had to explain what she was doing here. Guests weren't scarce to the Triple M, but female guests attached to him were. Not that Linc didn't like the ladies. But he liked even better to keep his personal life private.

He hurried to manage the introductions as all of them came together and the dogs quieted down. "Rachel, I'd like you to meet the best housekeeper and all around troubleshooter in the business, Linda Amato. She keeps this place humming whether I'm training my horses here or traveling on a buying trip. Linda, this is Rachel."

"Hi, Rachel," Linda said, brushing back her salt and pepper curls and beaming a smile outlined in cheery red lipstick. She extended her hand, jangling the silver bracelets on her wrist.

Much impressed by Linda's warmth and style, Rachel shook the hand and curtsied, too. "I'm very pleased to meet you, Linda."

Linc gestured to Bud. "This is my foreman, Bud Sylvester. He sees to the day-to-day operations of the ranch."

Bud removed his battered straw cowboy hat from his silvered hair and nodded his head. "How 'do, ma'am."

Rachel shook hands without curtseying this time, much to Linc's relief. "I'm pleased to meet you, Mr. Sylvester."

Without missing a beat, Linc draped his arm around Rachel's shoulders. "If you're going to call him that, then he better call you Mrs. Monroe."

Clapping her hands to her mouth, Linda squealed

in excitement. Bud scratched his head, looking from Linda to Rachel to Linc. "Naw. Can't be."

"My wife," Linc confirmed, taking perverse satisfaction in seeing Bud's mouth drop open in shock. Very little surprised Bud. And Linda usually had a pretty calm head on her shoulders. But not today.

"Congratulations," Linda cried, pumping Rachel's hand up and down. "It's about time Lincoln Monroe settled down and decided to be happy."

Linc forestalled more ridiculous outbursts by squeezing Rachel's shoulders. "Before the Missus and I go inside the house and enjoy the really happy part, there's plenty of work that needs doing. Bud, I picked up fifty head of working cattle and a real beaut of an untried filly. She's in the trailer, if you want to take a look. Linda, don't worry about supper for Rachel and me. I do need you to make up the master bedroom, though, please."

Linda bustled away immediately, while Bud appeared to have eyes for Rachel only. "Well, I'll be damn—Jim Dandy. Congratulations, little lady. I wonder if you could oblige me with the story of how—"

"She's had a long day, Bud," Linc cut in. "Get ready to unload the filly while I show Rachel into the house."

"But there's so much to see," she answered, swinging away toward the barn. By the time Linc explained what he wanted from Bud and caught up with Rachel, she was well inside the barn, her head tipped back to check out he-knew-not-what. "Goodness gracious. I've never seen so many stalls in one barn before. You didn't tell me you had a horse operation."

He took her elbow and firmly reversed her direction, propelling her back the way she had come. "I didn't tell you for a reason. It's none of your business."

"Certainly you can't blame me for my curiosity."

He figured there was no harm in humoring her as long as she kept moving. "I made a name for myself ropin' and ridin' in rodeos. Now that I'm retired, folks have taken to hiring me to train their horses."

"Is that why you bought the filly...to train her for someone else?"

"Not exactly. I may keep her for myself, depending on how she turns out."

"Thank heavens you found me to help." Rachel paused to rub the nose of the gelding in the stall nearest the door. "The filly is intelligent and well conformed, but unschooled."

"Rachel, the last thing I need—"

"Goodness gracious," she exclaimed, rising up on the tips of her shoes to better see over the nearest stall door. "That broodmare is about ready to burst."

"She's carrying twins," he said dryly, knowing exactly what Rachel was up to. Question was, how to handle it. She wouldn't take no for an answer.

"The mare needs looking after. I can't believe you would leave her alone."

"I have five cowhands who live here full-time—more in calving season. Bud sees to it that all my stock gets the attention it needs."

"Five men aside from you? How many cattle do you run?"

"Give or take a thousand," he replied, forestalling her next question by propelling her out into the yard. "I'm sure you must be tired. The front door of the ranch house is open. It's time you looked around in there."

"Aren't you going to unload the filly?"

"Bud and I will take care of it."

"But—"

"Rachel," he interrupted, his tone full of implied warning. "Remember our little discussion on cooperation?"

"*Cooperation* implies working together. Where would you like me to be when you unload Summer?"

"On the front porch of the house," Linc replied. "Going inside. All I want from you is a couple of minutes of blind obedience."

There was the humor, lurking under his soft, dead-pan delivery. At least she hoped it was humor. If not, her next words would be like waving a handkerchief in the face of an angry bull. "It won't be blind. I'll be watching from the porch. I want to see how Summer handles you."

The corner of his mouth may have twitched. She wasn't sure. His rugged face didn't lend itself to easy reading. What she noticed were the intimidating strides that ate up the ground between the porch and the trailer. He grabbed a lariat from the bed of his truck and motioned to Bud.

Linc tied a short rope to the trailer door, then set the looped lariat in the crook of his arm. He readied the rest between his gloved hands for what she assumed would be a throw. He obviously thought Summer was going to come flying out of that trailer like a bat out of hell.

He was right. He signaled Bud with a quick nod, then yanked the trailer door open. Rachel saw Summer's rump bunch as she tried to kick and back out of the trailer at the same time. Whinnying in fear, she banged sideways a couple of times, visibly shaking the trailer.

Linc grabbed the lead rope and hung on but the horse was terrified, and Bud jumped to grab Summer's ear in a desperate attempt to control her. She lunged, snapping at his hand. Rachel sprinted across the yard, yelling and waving her arms, distracting Summer long enough to where Linc retained control. He forced her into a tight circle, pulling her out of everyone's way.

It worked, but just barely. Prancing in nervousness, she wanted to have her head, and kept fighting the lead rope.

"Ornery, ain't she?" Bud shouted.

She's not the only one, Linc thought, seeing Rachel out of the corner of his eye. "Get the truck out of the corral," he told Bud.

Rachel opened the gate just enough for Bud to drive the truck out, then quickly slammed the gate shut. Linc had to concede it was a good thing she was there. The wind had kicked up, and she made sure the gate didn't clink and clang around scaring Summer further.

"Let her go, Linc," Rachel implored. "Please let her go."

Along with the wind-whipped dress, her hair, despite her braids, was windblown, too, with the wisps Linc had noticed earlier catching the gold from the sunset. The crinkling of her eyes against the wind didn't stop their blue from sparkling in the sun, either. It was altogether too vivid a picture, reminding him that if she had a lick of sense, she wouldn't have convinced him to bring her here in the first place.

Once he did let Summer go, she dashed the length of the corral, shrieking in fear. He clambered over the fence before she came tearing back at a fast gallop. A couple of mares from his working herd whinnied in greeting. Summer stopped on a dime, her ears swiveling every which way, and despite the steady wind, Linc heard Rachel's whistle. "Poor girl doesn't know what to think."

"Yeah? Well, I know what I think about you running in, waving your arms like a helicopter gone loco. You could have gotten yourself killed."

"Summer is scared, not vicious. What's a helicopter?"

"Don't try to change the subject. As long as you're on my ranch, I'm responsible for you. Do what I say next time. Got that?"

"Yes, Linc. Now please tell me what a helicopter is."

"It will be in tomorrow's lesson plan," he informed her, certain that she hadn't heard the point he was trying to make.

Determined to see her to the front door this time,

he gripped her elbow, unceremoniously ushering her toward the house. "Keep an eye on her," he told Bud.

"The horse or the missus?"

"Funny, Bud. Very funny."

Bud tipped his hat to Rachel. "Nice to meet you, Rachel. Can't wait to hear the story of how you two met."

"Don't hold your breath," Linc told him. "She's going to be too busy to do much talking in the next few days."

"Bet you will be, too, Boss," Bud said with a wink.

It dawned on Rachel what he was talking about, and she checked Linc's face, feeling the red burning her own. As if he couldn't wait to make her "too busy," he hurried her toward the house.

"What about my belongings?" she asked.

"You're my wife," he said, "and my wife understands that she leaves the loading and unloading to her husband."

Nervous about the prospect of being alone in the house with him before she was prepared, Rachel halted at the bottom of the porch stairs. "I'd be happy to help you take my saddle to the barn," she said brightly.

"The only thing you need to worry about is getting that cute little rump of yours into the house."

"Oh, dear."

"'Oh, dear' is right. Get moving."

He opened the door. She dallied again. Herding her from behind, Linc spoke directly into her ear. "Remember...obey?"

Still she hesitated. Linc realized she must be waiting for him to carry her over the threshold. Since he was being so insistent about her following the letter of the law regarding her obedience to their wedding vows, he scooped her up and pushed his way inside. "What are you doing?" she gasped

"I'm carrying you over the threshold."

She had a fair amount of heft, a strength that showed itself as she stiffened in his arms. And that baby-fine hair of hers had loosened. Several long locks had fallen across her face. He set her down in the front room, itching to tuck the hair behind her ears. "Instead of carrying you inside, maybe I should have given you a swift kick to your cute, little rump."

"You wouldn't do that. You're much too nice."

"'Nice,' huh?" This time he didn't stop himself from reaching for that lock of hair. But he didn't tuck it behind her ear. He tugged it, not hard, but none too gently, either. "What do I have to do to prove that you have way too high an opinion of me?"

He wound her hair around his finger and hungrily stared at her mouth.

"Do I have your attention?"

She nodded. "You will always have my attention, Linc."

"I was beginning to wonder." He was beginning to wonder about a lot of things. Like how incredibly soft her hair was. Had it been that way since she was a little girl? And her eyes. How could the color change from cornflower blue to violet in seconds?

She must have noticed his intense interest because she began to act just a teensy bit nervous. She snagged her lower lip with her front teeth and raked her loosened hair back, preparing to refasten it to the back of her head.

"Don't," he said. "Let it go."

Rachel felt her hands freeze in place. "It?"

"Your hair," he said and, reaching behind her, plucked out a wayward hairpin. He held it up in front of her face, then deliberately let it drop to the floor.

Her composure slipping, Rachel swallowed down her apprehension. After all, he hadn't threatened her in the least. "But a woman may only let down her hair for her husband."

This amused him, hooking one side of his mouth and upward crinkling his expressive eyes at the corners. "Don't I qualify?"

"I wasn't thinking. Goodness gracious. Of course. Yes. Let me just—" Her cute little rump, as he put it, thumped against the closed door as she backed into it. She lowered her head to better reach the pins holding her braids.

"Let me," he said, reaching behind her. Pins pinged on the wooden plank floor.

Her hair began to slip from its moorings, prickling her scalp and drying her throat, unwinding and falling over her shoulders. Featherlight was his touch, which she found difficult to imagine, given the broad strength of his hands, yet imagining was all she was capable of, for she closed her eyes to better feel the abrupt but delicious melting going on between her flesh and her bones.

She had never shown the full length of her hair to anyone before. It was the one possession that she'd had the luxury of keeping entirely for herself. To share it now forced her to realize the reality of what she had undertaken, of what marriage to him meant.

She would have to share herself. Yet she had no assurance that he would do the same. Why should he? He hardly knew her. Perhaps she hardly knew him, either, but the situation was more complicated for her. She had agreed to marry him of her own free will. She'd agreed to leave the only place she had ever lived to come here with him, too, and that implied a certain faith, a certain willingness to accept his overtures.

He picked up the length of her hair with both hands. Smoothing it down the front of her gown, his knuckles grazed the slope of her breasts. She opened her mouth to protest the intimacy, then realized she should have prepared herself for it. He was entitled. And he appeared to realize it, too. One side of his mouth curved into a very lazy grin. "Feeling a little hot under that collar, Rachel?"

"I am," she admitted.

The admission tugged at his smile, turning it wry, and his fingers went to that collar. One slipped between it and her neck, skimming her throat until he found the top button of her collar. Fingering it open, he set his thumb against the exposed hollow at the base of her neck.

She quivered at the contact. His smile widened. Loosening the collar again, he slipped open another button and another, parting the material of her bodice as he went.

An involuntary spasm caused her to spread her

hand over her upper chest, halting what he was doing. He gazed at her face. "Am I moving a bit fast for you Rachel?"

The tender huskiness of his voice gave her leave to tell the truth. She nodded.

His face was mere inches away from hers. "Would you rather kiss instead?"

She nodded again, and her gaze touched his mouth. She moistened her lips with a nervous-kitten flick of her tongue. The sight satisfied his hope to keep her cowed and off balance, but behind the fly of his jeans he was growing uncomfortable. It didn't make him happy. Not when the last woman he wanted to be aroused by was his wife.

His gaze dropped to her mouth. Instinctively she sensed what he was going to do, that he was lowering his head to kiss her. She closed her eyes. Nervousness made her wet her lips. His breath, mint scented as before, cooled the moisture there. She felt how near he was, close enough that their bodies touched, sending gooseflesh over her.

Expectation squeezed her lungs. But holding her breath became impossible as more and more seconds ticked by. She supposed this was the nature of a private kiss between husband and wife, to wait and wait until her heart fluttered painfully and she could barely draw breath.

"Hey, Rachel," he murmured.

"Yes?" she whispered.

"Open your eyes."

"Why?"

"I'm your lord and master, remember?"

Her eyes flew open to see him smiling at her quite tenderly.

"I was just thinking we'd better not do this," he said.

"Pardon?"

"At least not right now. What's the old saying? Absence makes the stomach grow fonder?"

Although what he'd said made little sense, she didn't even blink. "But that's hearts."

"A valid point. But we left the auction around noon. You must be starving."

"Starving?"

"For food," he supplied, affected by how overwhelmed she was. He'd barely touched her. He stepped away from her. "Excuse me. I've forgotten my manners."

"Manners?" she echoed, dazed.

"Yes, manners."

He pressed his advantage, sprinting outside to retrieve her trunk. She was still standing where he left her when he came inside.

He eased the trunk down. It thumped on the solid plank floor. Everything in the house was built to take the worst kind of weather and punishment. Because of the nature of his business and the premium horses he trained, he entertained out-of-town owners and their guests on a regular basis. Owners of top-notch horses tended to be used to top-notch accommodations. That didn't mean his kind of comfort added up to their kind of luxury, though.

The floors were solid maple and the walls, split logs. Knotty with imperfections, the furniture was made from rough-hewn pine that still smelled freshly cut. Couches and chairs were upholstered in distressed natural leather or the reds, blues and ivories of Navaho blankets. He liked earthy-colored wool in his rugs, too, which were scattered liberally throughout the great room that served as the central living area and the upstairs balcony that overlooked the great room and led to six bedrooms.

Two floor-to-ceiling fireplaces, one in the great room and one in the large but cozy kitchen, were built without mortar from specially fitted rocks. Also in the kitchen, slabs of slate had been neatly cut to form countertops. The sink and appliances were stainless steel.

Since wealthy people hated to share anything, each bedroom had its own bath, generous in size and style. For the fixtures and tiles he had chosen clean white and deep pine-green, but each suite had its own personality, accented by colors ranging from masculine maroon to feminine pink, from yellow to tan.

The house impressed others but it also felt like home to him, and sometimes he wondered how a poor ol' boy from Texas had amassed the fortune necessary to buy the land and build the thing. But rodeoing had paid big on the national level, and if he'd learned one thing on the circuit, it was the power of showmanship. Coupled with talent, hard work and enough luck to stay in one piece, a cowboy could make some good money.

"Feel free to look around," he said, hanging his hat on a peg by the door.

He turned to find her gone, having shed her boots

under the bench by the door. He could hear her excitement, however, with numerous "my-goodnesses" and "bless-my-souls" coming, apparently, with every new sight there was to see.

He rubbed his chin to keep from smiling. If she was trying to sound cute, he wasn't buying it. This whole day had been a disaster. Her constant enthusiasm didn't help. Call her the worst kind of pest.

He couldn't fault her aliveness, though.

He found her bellied up to the bar in the great room, counting the many trophies and silver and gold belt buckles he'd won over the past ten years, set on rows of shelves that climbed the wall to the open-beamed ceiling.

Without warning she caught him around the neck and pressed her cheek against his chest. "I am so glad you were at the auction to buy me."

His hands rose automatically to fend her off, but she sounded so damn sincere he didn't have the heart. Quick as a wink she spun away, darted into the kitchen and pulled open the refrigerator door. She stood in front of it, checking the contents. "Bless my soul, what's this?"

After he identified plastic bottles of ketchup, mustard and salad dressing and a carton of orange juice, she held up two shiny aluminum cans. "Beer," he said. "Want one?"

"Heavens, no. I don't drink spirits."

Spirits. "Mind if I do?" He popped the top of the can before he noticed how she was looking at him, round-eyed with worry.

"You won't lose your head with drink, will you?"

"No, Rachel, I won't lose my head with drink."

She flitted from room to room while he ambled after her, either scratching his chin or taking swigs from his beer to keep from laughing outright. There was no telling what she might do.

Once they made it back to the kitchen, he turned on the hot water tap just to see her face change. "Goodness gracious," she said.

"Are you hungry?"

"I'm not a very good cook," she warned.

"But you do eat."

"Yes."

"Then I have nothing to worry about. Do you like stir-fried beef?"

The dish was unfamiliar to her. "I like beef," she said cautiously.

"Coming right up."

His cheerful declaration was enough for her to recover some humor, especially when it became apparent he knew his way around a kitchen. He rummaged through the refrigerator. Myriad vegetables began to appear on the counter. The beef he produced was a small tenderloin, which he sliced with eye popping speed. Chopping the vegetables was even faster. After finishing with each ingredient, he threw it into a bowl-like pot on top of the stove, which sizzled and steamed, sending intriguing scents into the air. She identified the smell of ginger but not much else.

She devised a series of questions to put herself more at ease with him, now that they were becoming acquainted in other ways, and began with harmless ones about the dish he was making. Linc wasn't much of a talker, but she persisted and found out he had grown up on a ranch in Texas, the youngest of three boys.

Encouraged to learn something of a personal nature about him, Rachel pressed for more information. "Does your family still live here?"

"My father does, alone. He's a stubborn old cuss. Won't ever leave, I expect."

"And your mother?"

He shrugged in an offhand manner. "She ran away when I was nine. Haven't seen her since."

"Ran away?" asked Rachel, unable to believe a mother would leave her children under any circumstances.

He sampled a bit of the mixture he was stirring. "Turned out to be a good thing. Mmm-mmm. Wait until you taste this. Give me your plate."

She handed it over, although her appetite had suddenly disappeared. "How can you say your mother's leaving was a good thing?"

Without missing a beat, he heaped on the food. "You know how it is. She and my father got tired of each other. They started to fight all the time. She was fed up with trying to scratch out a living in the middle of nowhere, I guess. The good thing about her leaving was that once she took off, I learned to depend on no one but myself." He rubbed his stomach and smacked his lips. "Had to learn to cook, for example. You're not the only one in the world who likes to eat."

Rachel looked down at her plate, biting back questions about how his father could let his family come to such a sad state of affairs. Linc's joking manner must hide a world of hurt. Pointing that out, however, would be unwise. Trust needed to be built before either one of them would be ready to reveal such deep feelings.

Focusing on her meal, she turned the subject, praising the wonderful taste of his concoction. She asked him how he came to buy his ranch. He mentioned his years in rodeo and the conversation flowed.

Rachel was well versed about the competitive nature of rodeo cowboys, but she wasn't aware of how popular the sport had become. Linc had been on the rodeo circuit for twelve years, then quit to start his own horse-training operation, finally settling on a ranch in Montana because he loved, of all things, the winter cold. He said he figured he'd stored up enough dry heat from growing up in West Texas that he couldn't tolerate any weather except cold.

Encouraged that he had opened up to her some, especially after his initial resistance, she leaned back in her chair and stifled a yawn.

"Time for bed?"

The question caught her by surprise, but she couldn't very well refuse. "Come on," he said. "More wonders await. Let me show you what's upstairs."

He showed her to a room with a giant bed. She tried not to look at it too often as he ambled around instructing her on how to switch on the lights and work the doors of her closet, one of two in the room, along with two matching chifforobes.

He seemed especially pleased to present the bathroom to her, and considering the relatively confining space, she began to see why. Every moment he seemed to be bumping into her or brushing by her. He flushed the indoor toilet and turned on the water in the sink, then the shower closet and then an extra-large washtub that she thought she might drown in. Perhaps that was his intention, because he turned on the taps and invited her to jump right in.

"With you here?" she asked.

"I'll give you some privacy. If you have trouble, call me," he said sternly.

"Yes, Linc."

He'd left his vest on the bar where the towels were hung. She picked it up and, struck by the softness of its inner flannel, rubbed it against her cheek. She identified the smell of sage and saddle soap underscored by hints of lemon, and an unidentifiable something she couldn't name. Sweet grass, she thought. Or the gentlest kind of rain.

Folding the shirt, she hurried to the bedroom and placed it on the chair where he could easily spot it when he returned. Cowardly it was, but she didn't want him looking for it in the room where she was bathing. Already embarrassment and the bright pink blush that went with it burned her face. If he happened to amble in while she was naked, she might turn red as a brick...all over. Goodness gracious, she would never recover from mortification.

She started the water going in the bath and, criss-crossing her arms over her middle, she hugged her waist, imagining what was in store for her tonight. Though moody, Linc had been gentle enough with his horses. She would make sure he was gentle enough with her.

She had dreamed of this moment, dreamed of being touched and even disrobed by a man. And to disrobe Linc Monroe—what would that be like? She felt the fantasy of his hands roaming over her. And what of her hands roaming over him?

She'd been taught the anatomy of men and the differences that set them apart. But there were some things that didn't make sense to her, and the superiority displayed by the married women of her acquaintance only made human biology that much more mysterious. She wasn't quite sure what to expect—she didn't have friends to tell her—but after a lifetime of watching animals in and out of the barnyard, Rachel assured herself that she had imagination enough to know what he expected of her. And the experience must be more than tolerable if mothers chose to have children more than once.

Linc said he would teach her. But she wished to be prepared for him so as to not look foolish or strange, as she'd so often been called in her growing up years. That had been before she'd given up trying to share her knowledge and fit in with the people and values of The Community.

Marveling at the steam rising from the tub and the ready flow of hot water that poured from its spout, she quickly disrobed and stepped in. Gasping at the deep warmth, she sank to her knees, cupping handfuls of water and bringing its heat to her face. Rivulets ran down her neck, leaving coolness behind. Shivering a bit, she sat back against the surround of the tub and let the world of warm water engulf her, sinking down until she floated and her hair swirled about her shoulders like feathers. Heaven, she thought. Heaven.

Presently she reached for the soap. It lathered quickly in her hands, making her heady with its scent of full-blown roses.

She even used the thick liquid in a bottle that Linc called shampoo. Made expressly for the cleansing of hair, she read, and worked it from scalp to the ends of her hair, amazed by the abundance of frothy lather. It reminded her of the shaving soap she had whisked for her father every morning before his recent death.

Refilling the tub and rinsing herself in fresh water was a luxury in and of itself. Unfortunately, when she stepped from the bath and toweled herself dry, her hair was tangled beyond recognition. The shampoo had left a heady fragrance, however, that made her decide that the extra combing out would be worthwhile.

Wrapping a towel around her shoulders and a second towel around her hips, she peeked into the bedroom. Gone was Linc's shirt, and the room was empty of his presence, too. She padded to the chifforobe to retrieve her nightclothes.

Many years ago, with what Rachel had perceived at the time to be wishful thinking, her mother had sewn a fine lawn nightgown for the future occasion of her wedding night. Lace ruffled the high neckline, and the bodice was yoked, sending a fall of pleats straight to the floor. Satin ribbons trimmed the hem and the wide, blouson sleeves, and Rachel held it up, feeling the love of her mother in the fine stitches and

the extravagance of handmade lace. Tears fell, but
Rachel dashed them away. She wasn't one for weep-
ing. But Mama had understood her as few had, indulging the delight she took in frilly things and feminine doodads as well as her desire to be in the great
outdoors, whether it be climbing a tree or quietly sewing her samplers beneath it.

With care, she ducked her head under the cloud of
material and let it float down, feeling the swirl of air
touch her body. Soon Linc would be touching her in
some of the same places.

Her fingers trembled as she tied the line of ribbons
in front that held the bodice together. He would be
untying the ribbons, too. Rachel swallowed and felt
how dry her mouth had become at the thought.

She waited for him in the rocking chair, but found
her head nodding after some time. What could be
keeping him? She knuckled her eyes, wishing she'd
slept better the previous night. In anticipation of the
auction, she had tossed and turned until her usual rising time of dawn.

She decided she had better wait in their bed rather
than suffer the embarrassment of having him find her
slumped and asleep in the chair. Yet once she lay
down, all sorts of thoughts sped through her mind.
Wicked thoughts.

She heard his footsteps in the hall and abruptly sat
up in bed, arranging the quilt around her waist. The
last thing she wanted was for him to think she was
frightened.

His steps paused. The slit of light under the door

went out, then she heard the muffled turn of the knob. Yet the door remained tightly shut.

Rachel held her breath. If she hadn't, she might have missed the creak of his step, treading, she sensed, past the door. Another door clicked shut, distantly, farther down the hall. He must have entered another room.

She listened for several minutes. There was the rushing sound of water through the indoor pipes and the faint scrape of a chair leg or table leg. Or a bedstead, she realized, in the silence following.

Eventually she crept from the bed. The other closet door slid open as easily as hers had when she'd unpacked her things. But the floor, the rod and the shelves within the closet were empty. She checked the drawers of the chifforobe, too, and realized the cold and numbing truth.

This room was solely hers.

Four

The first thing Linc noticed after he left his small back bedroom the next morning was that Rachel wasn't in her room. She'd left her door wide open as if she wanted him to know it, too. Worse, he smelled coffee. Burning coffee.

He pounded down the stairs, still closing the snaps on his shirt. Shadows darkened the front room, the breaking light of dawn barely pink through the windows. Artificial yellow spilled from the kitchen, though. And, thankfully, there was no telltale sign of smoke.

He found her sitting cross-legged on the floor, of all places, her hair in a long braid down her back, the gleam of freshly polished wood beneath her. She wore a plain white, button-down shirt and black pants—clothes like the ones he'd seen the men wear at The Community. The shirt was buttoned all the way to the neck, making her look like a boy. Her pants had the opposite effect, however, exposing the perfect proportions of her tiny waist and trim hips.

"Good morning, Linc."

"'Morning," he replied, unsure if it was good or not to find he was just as attracted to Rachel as he was yesterday. Maybe more so, since he seemed to be noticing the smallest details in her appearance.

Scowling, he tromped past her and checked the perfectly normal-looking coffee machine. A full pot was made. She must have spilled some coffee on the burner or, more likely, scoured the burner into renewed efficiency. The chrome on the other appliances glittered. Undercutting the smell of burned coffee was the smell of pungent ammonia. "You've obviously been busy this morning. But I didn't bring you here to clean for me."

"I'm afraid I'm a creature of habit." Stretching her legs out in front of her, she smoothed the fabric over the length of her legs. "That is, except for the wearing of skirts. I must say, my first experience in the wearing of trousers has taught me their practicality in doing household chores. I'm looking forward to testing them on out-of-doors chores as well."

"I didn't bring you here to do outside chores, either. You should—"

"I can't wait to meet your horses and ride," she interrupted, widening her legs in a full stretch. Excitement brightened her already-bright and incredibly blue eyes. "My skirts were so confining and now I may spread my legs as wide as I wish."

What little resemblance she had to a boy abruptly vanished at that point. The masculine pants outlined the roundedness of her curves. Small pointed feet peeked from the pant cuffs, pale delicate feet that would easily fit into the palm of his hand. Fit far too easily.

"Where did you find that get-up?"

"The trousers and shirt belonged to my father. He passed on last year," she added matter-of-factly.

"I'm sorry."

"I appreciate the kind words. He was a very good man. And fortunately, not a great deal taller than I am. I took the trousers in at the waist. They are a bit loose in the midsection but I think they'll do for working."

He didn't bother to comment on her archaic use of the word *midsection*. The less attention he drew to her waist, the better. "I already told you. I didn't bring you here to work for me."

"Surely I can be of some service to you."

The thought of her servicing him was what, unfortunately, he was afraid of. He really should tell her to get out of those clothes. But the clothes weren't the problem. The body inside them was, shaped too much like the fully mature woman she was. "What are you doing up so early?" he asked, bent on changing the subject. "It's barely daybreak."

"It's my favorite time of day. All is quiet and washed with the barest light of dawn."

Her lyrical description took him aback. He marveled at the depth of this seemingly simple woman before him. How often had he tried to put into words the beauty he saw in the ever-changing skies of Montana? Rachel summed it up in a single sentence.

"I hope you don't mind that I ventured outside," she continued. "I thought the filly might turn up lame this morning, what with all she went through yesterday. However, she appeared right as rain."

"You don't have to worry about the filly. I checked her out thoroughly last night after you went to bed."

She rose to her feet. "I wondered where you got off to. I suppose it was foolish of me, but I was waiting for you in my bed."

Her tone was light, as if she didn't particularly care one way or the other. But recalling his misleading behavior yesterday when he repeatedly came on to her, he sensed she did care, very much. She must have concluded that he had been turned off in some way and had changed his mind about consummating the marriage. Much as he wanted to keep her guessing about his motives in the sexual realm so she wouldn't forever be challenging him, it was wrong to reinforce the idea that this marriage was going to be anything other than temporary. "You're not being foolish, Rachel. But let me repeat. This marriage between us isn't real. We won't be sleeping together. You've got to remember that we hardly know each other."

"The knowing will come from sharing ourselves."

Irritated by the prospect of yet another argument, he rubbed the back of his neck. "This isn't a negotiation. I told you how things are going to be between us. End of discussion."

She fisted her hands on her hips. "Have I no say in this whatsoever?"

"No, you don't have a say in this," he said brusquely. "In fact, it's only out of the kindness of my heart that I'm allowing you to put off signing the annulment papers for this so-called marriage until you can make it on your own."

"'Make it'? What is *it?*"

"It's an expression. No, wait, *it* is not," he corrected, though the correction posed more of a problem. Rachel's pure look of bewilderment didn't help. She was only trying to understand. Why did he keep losing his temper with her? Calling for patience, he took a deep breath and gestured toward the seating area in the great room. "Sit down, and I'll try to explain."

She perched on the edge of one of the chairs. The zigzag Southwest design of the upholstery enriched her coloring, making her all the more pretty. Or maybe it was the way she sat, naturally erect and feminine, despite the clothes. "Well?" she asked.

He took the seat opposite her on the leather sofa and leaned toward her, intent on making his point. He didn't want to be charmed by her ignorance, whether it be about the ways of the world or the meaning of modern slang. He didn't want to admire her ready curiosity and he certainly didn't want to notice the intelligence that prompted it. Why did she have to be so charming and cute?

"I apologize if I misled you last night. I thought it would be easier on you to wait," he clipped.

Warmed by his thoughtfulness, Rachel softened. "You were trying to spare my feelings?"

"What else would I be trying to do?"

She mulled this over, aware of the importance of helping him feel comfortable with her. "My feelings are this. I am happy to be your wife—whether it is sharing a meal or sharing a bed."

"Don't forget," he admonished. "You're going out on your own soon, remember?"

"Until then, I am still your wife."

"I teach, you learn. That's the extent of our relationship—and that's stretching it."

One glance at the forbidding angle of his brow told Rachel that he meant to chastise rather than compliment her. But she wasn't one to be easily chastised.

She sprang to her feet. "I made coffee. Would you like some?"

"Sure," he said, although his nose told him he might regret it. But he felt bad about coming down on her so hard. He was certain she'd been taught that finding a husband would put an end to all her problems. He didn't feel good about the role he needed to play to let her see the error of such thinking, but she wouldn't survive on her own otherwise.

Quick as a wink she filled a mug and handed it to him. Little grains of coffee floated on top of the weak, brown brew. "Thanks," he said.

"You're welcome." She beamed, her eyes tilting mischievously at the corners.

Unwilling though he was to let her get to him, she was getting to him. "Have you eaten yet?"

"I made biscuits." She showed him the basket

she'd covered with a blue gingham napkin. He peeled it back. Inside nestled a good ten or so crusty dark brown circles dusted with flour.

"Yum."

"Near burned to a crisp as they are, I'm surprised to hear you say that. As I mentioned, I'm not a very good cook."

"You don't have to be. There are plenty of pre-pared meals available in the supermarket. And for your information, it's not always up to women to pre-pare the food. First lesson of the day—you shouldn't give a guy the time of day if he doesn't know how to put a good meal together."

"Now I understand," she said, shades of silver twinkling from her eyes. "That explains your prowess in the kitchen."

Bent on resurrecting a strictly impersonal approach with her, he abruptly set the coffee mug down. "It's time you learned the ropes around here. Feel free to explore the house. I'll come back for you later."

"Where are you off to?"

"I'll be outside doing chores."

"May I help?"

He hesitated, aware of how winsome she looked and that she was asking him this time. With effort he reminded himself it wasn't fair to encourage her. "You might as well know I'm a bear in the mornings. Stay here and you won't find out how bad it can be."

"You're a bear whatever the hour," Rachel re-plied, picking up his abandoned coffee cup. "Now where are the ropes? I mean to start learning them first thing."

She glanced at him inquiringly, but he seemed to be taking a new interest in her biscuits, rubbing at his jaw, his shoulders shaking in the most suspicious fashion. "Are you laughing at me?"

He sobered instantly, showing her that distancing look in his eyes, the look she was coming to recognize far too well. "Don't worry about any ropes. I'm leaving strict orders for you to watch television this morning. I'm betting it will open your eyes to a whole new world."

"I've heard of television. Families that join as new members to The Community often complain of its existence."

"Judge it for yourself." He strode to what looked to be a big black window in the front room. Jabbing at it with his fingers, he caused a picture to appear behind the glass. Moving pictures.

Fascinated, she halted beside him. "I don't understand what I'm seeing."

"You've seen photographs, haven't you?"

"We were not supposed to, except in books. But my father liked to read newspapers and magazines. He would pay an outsider with land bordering ours to smuggle them in to him. I see you have a number of magazines here. May I borrow some?"

"They're all yours. Now, what you are seeing on television is sort of a series of photographs that are taken by a special camera. Then the photographs are strung together into film. Film shows continuous action."

She glanced at the black box. "I will show you by my actions what a help I will be to you."

"Rachel, this isn't The Community. People don't have to spend every waking moment working to survive. Take some time off. You've earned it."

"Ah, Linc. You have no idea how much I've indulged myself already in the short time I've been here. To step into the most comfortable home imaginable, to eat food prepared by another, to sleep in a warm bed.... I am so grateful to you." She kissed him. His hand grazed her waist, then was gone as he stepped back. She shivered all the same.

Before she could say more, he headed for the door, spurs jangling on the polished floor.

Rachel decided an hour and a half later that the world presented on television appeared fraught with difficulties, real and imagined. There was much talk, with sounds of raucous music, continuous applause or hearty laughter at the slightest provocation.

As open as her eyes were, she didn't understand what the fuss was all about. As educational as Linc thought television to be, the call of the outdoors was just too strong for Rachel to resist. Although Linc had been kind enough to point out the ranch buildings, she wished to sort them out by daylight and discover what lay inside them. Certainly such an endeavor was as informative as what was on TV.

Nevertheless, she was careful to keep from his sight, at least until she'd seen her fill.

The buildings reflected his no-nonsense attitude. Facing east, the animal pens adjoining them faced south, affording the animals more warmth in the winter. Most of the pens were empty, except for a couple of cows with their calves. She found a long stick and gave their backs a good long scratch.

The chicken coop was boarded up, the wire enclosure weedy with wild grass. Though it was a smelly, dirty job, she didn't much mind the caring of a chicken coop. The horizontal slats that made up the walls enchanted her with the pale light they let in, picking up tiny particles that lived in the air. She had years ago given up her game of catching them, but the flap of chicken wings left floating feathers, and she'd often had the treat of pulling them off her clothes and hair and blowing them to the four winds.

The cattle fed as cattle fed everywhere, noses burrowed in the hay, unconcerned about the world around them. But it was the horses that drew her as they always did. She was impressed by the quality and quantity of Linc's herd, counting twenty-two animals in all, mostly mares with young ones. In the absence of a stallion, the lead mare dominated.

Summer, the filly Linc had purchased yesterday, remained in the round pen. Separated from the herd, she could nevertheless hear and smell its presence. The possibility of new acquaintances agitated her, and Rachel spent long moments watching, sensing it was too soon for her to approach. Just as she herself needed time to adjust to the new surroundings, the filly needed time to adjust.

Kept separate in a far-off field were three draft horses. The only person between her and them was Bud, who was moving some steers from one pen into another. She waved as she walked by, clear purpose in her step, as though her destination was condoned by Linc. Bud tipped his hat but didn't deter her.

As she neared the fence, the draft horses started forward to greet her. She leaned against the horizontal poles of the fence and held out her hand. One of the huge horses nudged it, blowing his ready acceptance of her through his nose. The other two did the same, jostling each other, vying for her attention. She nickered to them. They nickered back, bobbing their heads as if they completely understood the welcome she wished them.

She climbed through the fence to stand and stroke massive bodies that easily outweighed her, twenty-to-one. Yet they stepped delicately around her. Finally she petted each one in turn, becoming fully acquainted with nose rubs and soft words. Naming them for an old nursery rhyme, Wynken, Blynken and Nod, each came when she called.

She didn't know why this magic of communing so easily with animals happened to her. But her gift hadn't been appreciated in The Community. Trickery, people called it. Certainly her methods were not in keeping with the ways of old. And the people shunned her for it.

Remembering, Rachel felt the hurt of past rejection. Her new friends seemed to sense her distress, and Blynken sidled alongside her. She took his invitation and, grabbing a good handful of silvery mane, clambered onboard, pulling herself into a sitting position astride him.

The world looked full of new possibilities from high off the ground. Blynken pranced about, showing his pride. She hupped to him, and his ears swiveled, asking her what she wanted of him. She settled her seat, and he stepped out with his head up and his ears pricked forward. She let him jog around his friends for a bit, then calmed him into a walk until all three horses resumed grazing. Except for a chosen few, horses liked to be followers rather than leaders, especially this kind of personality—ever ready to pull his weight and work as a team. She lay back until her head rested on his broad rump and watched the clouds skid along the sky.

She must have nodded off, for an angry shout jolted her into sudden wakefulness. Galloping hooves thundered in her ears. She jerked upright into a sitting position and got an impression of blurred denim.

"What the hell do you think you're doing?"

The skidding to a stop of Linc's horse coupled with the commanding boom of Linc's voice startled Blynken. Rachel whoaed him to a halt. Embarrassed to be found dreaming, she moved automatically to right her skirts. Unfortunately she had forgotten she was wearing trousers rather than skirts, and in her self-consciousness, she answered more sharply than intended.

"Shouting scares these creatures."

Under the black brim of his cowboy hat, Linc's brows beetled into straight angry lines. "Who said you could get anywhere near them? These are Clydesdales, for God's sake. One hoof is enough to crush your head."

"As you can plainly see, my head is fine. And I

would ask you not to take the Lord's name in vain."
She met his scowl with one of her own.

"Do you know the problem I would have on my
hands if you broke your damn neck falling off one of
these horses? Who in their right mind would consider
riding a draft horse bareback? My God, how long
have you been out here?" he barked, not paying the
least attention to her suggestion to watch his language. "Did you even give television a chance?"

"Of course. *Jeopardy* is an answer and question
contest, although who is jeopardized I don't know.
Only the very fortunate spin the *Wheel of Fortune,*
and *Cable News* doesn't talk about cables at all."

Her neat summation of the hazards of daytime TV
raised Linc's smile, though he'd be damned if he
showed it. She appeared to be fully calm and col-
lected, which only angered him more. "Don't try and
change the subject. You're supposed to be in the
house watching television."

"I'd rather watch the clouds."

"Watching clouds using the back of a horse as a
lounge chair?" he asked sarcastically. "Don't you
think that's a little strange?"

"No, it's not strange," she said defensively. "If
you only tried it, you'd find how enjoyable watching
clouds from the back of a horse can be."

Within Linc's chest stirred an old memory. A
memory of a daydreaming small boy lying on his
back in the tall, dry Texas grass of summer, his arms
folded behind his head, imagining animal shapes and
heavenly bodies in the cottony clouds above. Hidden

from the world, no one could hurt him in the sun-baked garden of his own making.

But Rachel hadn't been hidden. From two pastures over, he'd spotted her figure on top of the horse because of that vivid combination of black pants and white shirt. But it was the spill of sun-like hair falling down over the Clydesdale's hindquarters that had scared the living daylights out of him. His gallop across the field had seemed to take forever. And here she was, in perfect health, pert and beyond pretty, defying him once again.

"Mount up behind me. I'm taking you home."

She shrugged and slid off the huge Clydesdale, kicking up dust in her jump to the ground. Twisting his neck, the Clydesdale snuffled the top of her head. Laughter pealed from Rachel, the kind of laughter that was intoxicating as well as infectious. With effort, Linc resisted the urge to chuckle. She needed to understand how much trouble she was making for him.

He extended his hand and clicked his fingers, gesturing at her to hurry to his side. "Come on, Mrs. Monroe. I've got work to do."

"Blynken wants to say goodbye first," Rachel said, scratching the whiskered chin of the huge horse.

"Blynken?"

"I didn't know what you called him, so I named him after one of my favorite nursery rhymes. Have you ever heard it?"

"Maybe, but too long ago to remember," Linc muttered, distracted by the way "Blynken" was chewing and moving his lips as if he really was saying goodbye to Rachel. Retreating a step, she waved her hand in front of the horse's eyes. "See you tomorrow."

Linc scowled at the sight. The woman had to have a screw loose. "Rachel, would you please get over here?"

"Of course, Linc," she said cheerfully, and sauntered over as though she wasn't aware of the fact that she had kept him waiting for a good deal longer than necessary.

Linc grasped her small hand and wondered again how a woman as delicately made as Rachel could possibly survive outside The Community. He swung her to sit in the saddle behind him, but since he outweighed her so much, he practically tossed her over the rump of the horse instead. Snagging his waist to stay upright, she laughed in delight. "When you want to take me for a ride, you really take me for a ride, don't you?"

An immediate fantasy played through his head of taking her on the most pleasurable of pleasure rides, the sort of ride that a man and a woman gave each other, preferably on a comfortable bed rather than on the bony back of a horse. Considering the soft feel of Rachel's breasts, however, Linc didn't think he'd have any trouble giving her all the pleasure she could stand and then taking the same from her, horse or not.

"Hold on to me tight," he ordered, forcing the fantasy from his mind. "I'm taking you home."

Rachel locked her arms around his waist and snugged her body close to his in the saddle. "Home. I like the sound of that."

Linc spurred his horse into a fast, ground-eating lope. Not only did he feel her breasts flattened intimately against him, he was aware of her thighs pressed against his, as well, rocking in rhythmic motion with his. The saddle horn mashing him below his belt buckle was the only thing that saved him. Severe groin pain did that to a man. But he couldn't depend on pain forever, whether it was physical or the pain in the butt that Rachel was turning out to be. He'd have to push her to learn as fast as possible or he was bound to take certain phrases of those marriage vows far too literally. Like to have and to hold in the most intimate embrace possible—as many times as she would let him.

Five

By the time she and Linc had made the short ride into the ranch yard, Rachel felt she had thoroughly capitalized on her first opportunity to show Linc how compatible they were. They shared an affinity for Montana's wide-open land and a healthy respect for the many creatures that lived upon it. Surely he would see how such commonalities led to the most successful of marriages. Her parents had shared similar interests and lived together for many years in perfect harmony. All she had to do, Rachel was sure, was to prove her value to Linc, whether it be in the form of showing her desire to heed his word and adjust to her new life as quickly as possible or to show a more obvious willingness to perform all the duties expected of a loving wife.

As they rode into the dusty yard between the house and the barn, Rachel gave Linc an extra squeeze around the waist. He'd shown kindness for her in giving her a ride back home with him. If he'd been truly angered by her escape from the confines of the house, he wouldn't have been nearly so understanding.

With the grace of a supremely confident male animal, he dismounted and reached to help her down from the saddle. The tingling at the touch of his strong hands at her waist led her to smile at him invitingly. She wasn't certain how to go about letting him know how willing she was to share the same bed with him, but she was certain that she had to be more frank about her intentions than she had dared to be on their wedding night.

Beneath the brim of his hat, his eyebrows drew together in a damning frown. "Don't look at me like I'm a piece of your favorite candy," he said.

"I wish to tell you how much I enjoyed riding with you. May we do it again soon?"

Not in this lifetime, Linc muttered to himself. "All I want you to worry about is getting ready to move into town sooner, rather than later. I'm taking my horse into the barn to cool down. When I come back I want to see you with your shoes on, ready to go over to Bud and Linda's house so that Linda can find you some jeans to wear. Your father's pants won't do, and, women haven't worn long dresses like yours for a good long time."

"I would like that very much. I want to wear the same kind of clothes that you wear—jeans and snap-button shirts."

"Right."

"Exactly right." Rachel made a note to ask for Linda's help in altering her gowns into more modern attire.

While searching for her shoes, Rachel recalled she'd left them by the fence that enclosed the corral penning her three newest friends—the Clydesdales. If she hurried back there, she could retrieve her shoes before Linc returned and found her cooperation wanting again.

She raced from the house, avoiding the barn. Bud was still working in the farthest corral, but since he hadn't stopped her in her wanderings before, he had no reason to now. And he didn't stop her. She stopped herself, horrified by what she saw.

A horse stood terrified in the nearest corner of the corral. A previously golden young filly, now lathered in dark sweat with her flanks heaving, held tightly to one spot by several ropes stretching out from thick knots tied around her neck. Summer was hardly recognizable. All the fight had been beaten out of her.

"My God, no!" Rachel ducked between the rungs of the fence, intent on rescue.

Summer lashed out, kicking and bucking, frenzied. Rachel retreated with tears in her eyes, realizing she could do little else. The horse was mad with fear and pain. Rachel recognized Bud's lariat coiled neatly in the middle of the corral with his working gloves laid on top. He had obviously gone on to do other things until the moment came when Summer wore herself out and submitted.

Rachel stretched out her hand, but Summer

squealed in panic and lashed out again. Her formerly intelligent eyes were ringed with white, showing how out of control she truly was. Rachel knew that even if she managed to get close enough to untie the ropes, Summer was liable to hurt herself unless otherwise confined. In a corral as large as this one, keeping her still and relatively calm was likely to be well-nigh impossible. The best solution at this point was to prevent Bud from coming back and finishing what he had begun.

Rachel dashed inside the barn. "Linc!"

Curry comb in hand, he appeared instantly at the door of his horse's stall. "Rachel, what is it? What happened? Are you all right?"

"Come quick. Something terrible has happened to Summer."

"Isn't Bud out there? He was supposed to be working on gentling the filly all afternoon."

"Gentling her! He has hobbled her to the point where she can't move."

Linc's long strides halted. "So? That's his job."

Rachel spread out her hands, pleading with him. "Every instinct inside a horse tells her to run when she's frightened and in danger, to run for her very life. Otherwise, she can't escape from her natural enemies, predators and the like. She wouldn't survive. Don't you understand? Bud has tied Summer down to within an inch of her life. He is preventing her from doing what comes naturally. He will break her spirit."

"That's the general idea. A horse needs to be broken in order to be ridden and trained."

"Not broken this way. Please, Linc. Summer's spirit is precious, as precious as any other creature's, including yours and mine. Bud and your other hands must be prevented from doing this to your horses. Cruelty can't be justified for any reason."

"Bud's a seasoned wrangler who's been breaking horses for some forty years. It's the way his father did it and his grandfather before him. Most important of all are the results. The owners I work for expect me to train their horses the same way mine were trained when I was winning all those rodeo titles. I can't change the way I run my outfit—my reputation depends on it."

"Are all traditions right and true? Do you still brand cattle with white-hot irons?"

"That's different."

"How?"

"Damn it, Rachel—"

"Damn it, Linc," she echoed, overlooking his increasing irritation. "How is it different?" she pressed, hands on her hips. Much as she wished to impress him with her ability to be his partner and helpmate, her feelings on this subject were far too important to allow him to intimidate her into silence. Even though he was her husband.

"It doesn't matter how the two situations are different," he retorted. "The point is, Bud works for me, not you. This is my business—and don't think you can stick your pretty little nose in it just because you corraled me into being your husband."

"I thought you were the one who trained these horses."

He returned to brushing the chestnut as if dismissing her. "I take over after Bud gets them to accept the saddle and bridle."

"How long does that take?"

He lifted one shoulder in a dismissive shrug. "A few weeks."

"I will bring the filly to saddle and bridle in one week," she challenged.

He cut her an exasperated look. "You're trying to do too much around here already. Now you want to take Bud's job? And with some pretty outlandish claims, to boot. Sorry, Rachel. I don't think so."

She tried to disarm him with a smile. "What I propose is not outlandish. All I wish is an opportunity to prove it."

"Even if I believed you could do it, Bud is my foreman. I won't undercut his authority in that way."

She touched his arm in a conciliatory gesture. "What about my authority?" she asked softly. "I am new to this ranch, and I am your wife."

He frowned. "A wife in name only."

"The filly comes from The Community. Does it not make sense to allow someone from The Community to work with her?"

"She's dangerous, Rachel. You saw how difficult it was to get her into the round pen when we arrived."

"What I saw was a creature made wary and frightened by all the newness around her. It is something I, too, have experienced lately."

Damn, she was fierce. Indignation pursed her lips and spiked her eyes. Behind them was passion, the kind of passion he once possessed long ago. It had driven him to practice his roping and riding skills and join the rodeo. It had driven him to save his money in order to buy his own ranch. Either way, he went after fame and fortune with a vengeance.

His determination to make his own way in the world extended into the rodeo ring. On the circuit, he performed best in the individual events: bull riding, bronc busting, cutting, reining and roping, and let his steady climb up the professional ranks do his advertising for him. He felt driven to succeed without help, training his own horses, hauling them from town to town himself until he and Bud hooked up.

Eventually, fame and fortune had come along, providing him with the means to retire. Buying his own ranch became his passion then. His success in rodeo gave him the name recognition he needed to clinch his reputation as the best trainer of western pleasure horses in the country. Even in Montana's back country, owners came to his ranch in droves.

But the satisfaction he should have felt when he attained his goals wasn't there. For some time now, he hadn't felt passionate about anything, unless he counted his roller-coaster obsession with Rachel.

With her firmly stated opinion still hanging in the air, Linc sent her a look of measured thoughtfulness, as though he was thinking over what she had said. He scanned the view outside the window of the stall, and searched the horizon, seeing the emptiness rather than experiencing the peace he once found there.

As a boy, he used to love to haunt the hills, riding his most faithful friends, the scrub ponies and mustangs he'd raised by hand. With them he practiced cutting and roping, herding heifers and searching for lost calves.

Now Bud and the part-time ranch hands he'd hired did that, and he concentrated on maintaining his position by attracting wealthy owners who could afford the top cutting and reining horses he specialized in. He rarely laid his hand on a lariat anymore.

Rachel, on the other hand, couldn't be held back from all she wanted to see and do. In the short time she had been here, she tackled every challenge he gave her with enthusiasm, even though she obviously felt self-conscious about her ignorance.

Except now she was putting her fingers where they didn't belong. She was challenging Bud's training methods. In a roundabout way, Linc felt she was challenging him as well.

The woman had guts. Bringing a horse to accept a saddle and bridle was a difficult task, requiring courage, patience and the persistence of Job. Adolescent horses like Summer tended to be high energy and high strung, resulting in the possibility of serious injury to both the trainer and the animal even where safety was the highest priority.

Linc heard the ticking of the clock on the wall. Rachel had been astute enough to keep quiet long enough for him to think this through. "Promise me you'll be careful," he said.

"Oh, Linc." She clapped her hands and tucked her folded hands under her chin. "Thank you. I promise you won't be disappointed."

How could he be disappointed when presented by the sparkle of excitement brightening her eyes. He brushed the ever-present wisps of pale-gold off her forehead, feeling surprise at his enjoyment of the clear happiness shining from her face. He was enjoying how close she was, too. "Allowing the chance to gentle Summer will be my wedding gift to you. That's what I'll tell Bud, at any rate. He's going to be unhappy about having you interfere with what he considers his job. To throw him a bone, I'll tell him to keep tabs on you and your progress. The two of you should try to get along."

"I promise to ask for his help when I need it. Thank you again, Linc." Lifting on tiptoe, she bussed his cheek in another one of her apparently affectionate kisses. He caught her around the waist before she could retreat, thoroughly enjoying himself. "Do you go around kissing every guy who does you a favor?"

Basking in the glow of gratitude, she turned the full effect of her brightest smile on him. "Only you, Linc. Only you."

Linc personally released Summer from her bounds, using every trick he knew to ensure she wasn't injured. Rachel decided that before she began her gentling of Summer, the horse needed some time to recover from the trauma of being frightened and misused. She was turned out to pasture.

Over the next week, Rachel and Linc established a daily routine. Working together to complete his chores as early as possible, they spent the rest of the morning on her education in Life 101. Linc started her reading the daily newspaper and discussed much of its content with her, explaining what she didn't

understand. He spent long hours teaching her how to
use the telephone and computer. He brought Linda in
to help Rachel familiarize herself with all the modern
conveniences and encouraged the housekeeper to an-
ticipate Rachel's questions about clothes, makeup and
other "women stuff."

The afternoons became Rachel's time to do things
on her own, whether watching TV, surfing the net, or
wandering the ranch. If Bud happened to have a spare
moment, she went out of her way to consult him,
asking him to share his knowledge about all sorts of
things.

A few days later, a cold front moved in, building
dull clouds across most of the sky. Instinct told her
the time was right to begin her work with Summer.
Rachel couldn't explain why when she was questioned by Linc and Bud. They simply had to trust her,
she told them, to know what was best.

They wanted to watch the process. With the threat
of rain in the forecast, both recommended that the
session take place in the indoor exercise ring.

Rachel believed otherwise. Experiencing the new
environment of the indoor ring would threaten the
horse more than the worst of Mother Nature's
weather.

She instructed Bud to move Summer into the smallest outdoor round pen. There were to be no restraints
on the horse once released, no hobbling, no halter, no
rope around her neck, legs or head.

Bud grumbled about safety, but did as she asked.
Rachel felt her heart pound at the shining beauty of
the horse, the straight spine and deep chest, and the

spotted white Appaloosa blanket that covered her
hindquarters and dusted her hind legs. Her tail was
long and full for an Appaloosa and flagged hand-
somely whenever Summer galloped around the pen or
shied in fear, which in Rachel's judgment was far too
often.

Before she entered the pen, Rachel noted how
Summer swiveled her ears and jerked her nose up,
listening and scenting and sometimes whinnying in
distress. Up until a few days ago, the filly had been
raised in the safety of The Community herd. Although
largely domesticated, the broodmares and their young
were left alone. By the time the fillies and colts were
auctioned off at the end of their third year, they rarely
had been touched by human hands.

Summer showed the same behaviors as the wild
horses Rachel had studied when she was younger.
Horses felt safest in herds with their own kind, where
there was more protection from predators. As flight
animals, their instinct was to move away from the
slightest whiff of trouble.

There was little doubt in Rachel's mind that Summer was in flight, running away in the only way she
could in her limited space. Her abrupt shying and high
speed changes of direction were a result of the sights
and scents bombarding her. She was also searching
for her herd. The other horses at the ranch had not
accepted her yet.

It was Summer's herding instinct that Rachel used
in her gentling art. In a way she became a horse herself, two-legged perhaps, yet a creature to be trusted,

who spoke the very language that Summer best understood.

But Rachel wondered if Linc or Bud would understand the importance of her gift. Although Linc had granted her this chance, he had been reluctant to do so, and she feared he was merely humoring her because she would be at his ranch for only a little while longer. This was her best chance to impress him and convince him to change his mind about letting her go.

Because so much depended on her performance, Rachel had used some of her preparation time asking Linda for advice on what to wear in order to look as much like a modern horse trainer as possible.

Unearthing some outgrown jeans and plain leather chaps, Linda had quickly altered them to fit. It seemed scandalous the jeans hugged her hips so tightly. But Rachel compared the fit to those she saw in the magazines and conceded that Linda's judgment was entirely trustworthy.

Dressed as she was, Rachel felt Linc's gaze boring into her, judging her approach, her refusal of the lunge rope and rejection of the whip. Shaking his head in disbelief, Bud prevented Rachel from entering the round pen. "Sorry, ma'am. I can't let you go meet a rank animal with nothing to defend yerself but yer good looks."

She swung at Linc. "You promised."

Linc nodded, tightening his jaw at the idea of seeing her in such danger. The horse weighed ten times more than she did. But he had promised. "Let her in, Bud. Keep your lariat ready, though. And tie a shank to the gate in case we need to open it quick."

"Right, Boss."

Thank the Lord Rachel had sense to slip inside the pen without taking her eyes off Summer, sending the horse into an immediate gallop to the opposite side of the round pen. It had a diameter of fifty feet, less room for Rachel to maneuver in than Linc would have liked.

She walked to the center of the ring before the horse took off again, galloping around the perimeter, staying as far away from Rachel as possible.

Summer eventually tired, slowing to a nervous trot. By this time, Rachel appeared to be tired, too, or at least less than attentive. Once Summer slowed to a walk, however, Rachel clearly shifted, squaring her shoulders parallel to the horse's length, measuring its reaction.

It galloped again, circling the perimeter several times before it started trotting, bobbing its head in agitation. Rachel seemed to pay close attention only when Summer settled into a walk. The moment the horse relaxed, even a little bit, Rachel would square her shoulders and stare at the horse straight on, starting the cycle of flight all over again.

Over the years, Linc had attended several demonstrations by advocates of natural training, people the general public termed horse whisperers. He'd seen them do the same things that Rachel was doing to win the animal's trust. But he'd never seen the demonstration done in such silence. The only sound was the occasional slicing and pounding of Summer's hooves on the sandy ground. Linc's focus narrowed, struck by an awed prickling of his scalp at this dance going on before him.

Both horse and woman mirrored each other, reacting at the same moment. Despite the fact that Linc was acquainted with the signals Rachel must be using, they were flowing too fast to be readable. Her fluency extended into her movement, subtle as the highest levels of dressage, and Summer responded in kind, becoming more calm, more predictable. It was the predictability that got under Linc's skin.

"She's good," Bud commented.

"Too good," Linc murmured. Raising his voice, he called to Rachel. "Talk to us, Rachel. Tell us what you're doing."

Summer reacted to the exchange with another hard gallop. Skidding to a stop, she began walking around the pen until Rachel shifted her shoulders and locked her eye directly on the horse.

"I am telling her to flee, that I know how to speak her language. She will slow when I look away because the threat is reduced. If I face her squarely, she will take off again. See?"

Rachel demonstrated.

Summer had tired and her coat was sweat sheened. She shuffled around the perimeter of the pen. Rachel stayed in her less aggressive stance. "I know Summer is listening because she is walking slowly and trying to talk in her own way to me. Notice how she opens and closes her mouth. But I will not have won her trust until she lowers her head toward the ground. See, there it goes. She's telling me she is ready to be friends."

Rachel's prediction panned out. Summer dropped her head close to the ground and continued chewing as though at the bit. Rachel remained motionless even when Summer began to approach her.

Linc gripped the fence, his scalp prickling. Rachel made it look easy. And she was fast. He'd never seen anybody calm an uncontrollable horse as quickly.

Summer halted, nose to Rachel's shoulder. She stroked Summer's muzzle and the star between the horse's eyes. "She trusts me," Rachel said.

Showing the extent of the trust, Rachel worked her way from withers to flanks to hindquarters, rubbing them down, all without the horse making a peep of protest. Even being touched in the most vulnerable areas, beneath the belly and along the legs, appeared to soothe Summer rather than spook her.

"Amazing," Bud said.

"I'm not so sure," Linc said. "Summer comes from the same place Rachel does. She's probably worked with the horse before."

"Maybe. Maybe not. All I know is, that horse nearly ran over me yesterday. She's as green as they come. It would have taken me days—no, a good long week of getting my butt kicked—to do what yer little woman did in an afternoon."

"Thank you, Bud," said Rachel, arriving at the fence. At her shoulder, Summer followed like an enormous dog. "May I have a halter, please?"

Linc handed her the halter. Rachel pet the horse's head again and slipped it on. Linc measured the entire process with clear skepticism. "Tell me, Rachel.

When I bid on this horse, the auctioneer claimed she was untouched by human hands. Is that true?''

Anger rippled through Rachel. And a surprising amount of hurt. To have Linc doubt her now crushed her beyond reason. Nobody in The Community had believed what their eyes were telling them, either. They accused her of orchestrating such demonstrations, of practicing deceit, of trying to show off or make herself seem better than everyone else. ''If you think I've cheated somehow, I'll gentle another horse right now, one of your choice. How about your meanest stallion?''

Linc snorted. ''You're liable to get yourself killed if you think you can tame a rangy, half-wild horse with nothing but your good looks.''

Bud cut in, removing his hat deferentially. ''I believe you, Rachel. You're the best I've seen in all my years.''

''You're out of line, Bud.''

''Sorry, Boss. I didn't mean to say—''

''Sure you didn't,'' Linc interrupted evenly. ''My wife and I need to have a little discussion. Will you excuse us?''

Bud obeyed, jamming his cowboy hat on his head and striding for the barn. Rachel didn't know what to say. The fact that Bud had, in no uncertain terms, come to her aid gratified her. Yet it certainly didn't make up for Linc's attitude. ''You're being unfair to both Bud and me, Linc.''

''Am I? I'm willing to admit that Bud was right. You have a gift, Rachel. However, what I saw was a special connection with this horse. I want you to work

with her while you're here. Train her. But let me be
very clear. This doesn't negate our deal. Starting this
Friday, I'm taking you to Tall Timber so you can see
the town and figure out where you want to live. By
the end of this month, you're going to be a full-time
resident there.''

"I understand," Rachel said, echoing his crisp
tone, yet elated by the prospect of training Summer.
But there was an unnamed fear as well. Linc acknowledged her with a touch to the brim of his hat, then
strode away without another word.

Rachel tried to decide if the trepidation she felt
came from the animal nature he exhibited or the dead-
line he had given her. Maybe she was afraid of both.

Linc stood at the threshold of his office adjoining
the stables, arms folded in front of him, watching Rachel continue her training and gentling of Summer.
The horse was being put through her paces and
looked to be enjoying herself. He knew the feeling.
Educating Rachel about the blessings and dangers of
life in the real world was proving to be easier now
that she'd focused more of her attention on capturing
the heart of the filly rather than capturing him.

Oh, he still found himself drawn to his wife's genuine yet unconscious sexiness. And he still allowed
himself to indulge in explicit fantasies featuring her
in a starring role. Her husky laugh continued to disarm him. She still said goodness gracious endearingly
at the most ordinary events of modern-day living.

But Linc found if he concentrated on her less-
desirable traits, her loyalty to traditional values and

her stubborn desire to remain on the ranch, the conclusion was obvious and inevitable: any kind of relationship between them, sexual or otherwise, would result in heartache for her; consequently, he would feel guilty as hell.

Unfortunately, she just didn't have the experience to understand. Emotional support was not his style. He didn't like too many demands on his precious free time, either. Rachel had already proven how time-consuming and argumentative she could be. She was also as obstinate as a mule. To cap it all off she didn't have a clue about where he was coming from.

In her world, commitments were unquestionable and lifelong. Marriage meant forever. In spite of her agreement to the annulment once she was ready to move to town, Linc knew better than to believe that Rachel would give up her values and beliefs without a fight. In all likelihood Rachel was bound to come up with some reason she needed to stay at the ranch, at least for a little while longer. Then that little while would lead to a longer while, and pretty soon he would find himself trapped.

She did have a way of turning his life upside down. Because of her unpredictability, he might have to come down pretty hard on her to make Rachel understand that despite the fact that he'd become her husband, he really wasn't good marriage material. The annulment would then be the best option she had left.

But even if he had to throw her off with several more demonstrations of how randy, selfish and off-putting he was capable of being, he wasn't about to let her think she could expect anything more from him.

Rachel glanced down from where she stood on the kitchen table. What remained of her pale pink gown was being fitted to a much more contemporary look. A month ago, she wouldn't have believed that she would have allowed her best and favorite gown to be cut down in this way. But then she couldn't believe a month had gone by since she left The Community. Every day seemed to fly by faster and faster, especially since Linc had given her leave to train Summer. However, the speedy passage of time was not an excuse for missing Sunday services for an entire month. Neither was her lack of the right clothes to wear.

"Linda, are you certain the neckline of this dress should be lowered in such a scooped fashion?" Rachel tried to come up with the least offensive description possible. "I feel...uncovered."

"You are covered up just fine," Linda replied around a mouthful of pins. "We're altering this dress for you to wear to my church. Believe me, I wouldn't let you wear it if it wasn't appropriate."

Rachel snagged her lower lip in doubt as she studied her reflection in the hand held mirror. "I feel like my underwear will be revealed for all the world to see."

"It won't, trust me. Now all we have to do is raise the hem and sew up the seams of the sleeves we ripped out." Linda pinched the material that covered Rachel's shoulders to show the look of the new straps on the dress.

"So thin?"

"Probably not thin enough. You'll be wearing plenty more than some of the women in church, believe me. Nowadays it seems like anything goes. Besides our little congregation can't afford an air-conditioner. You want to wear material that is very cool and airy, like this lovely pale pink linen of yours. Last Sunday I wore a navy jersey and about roasted myself to death."

"I suppose that means I can't wear a sweater to cover my shoulders."

"Not unless you want half the county to think you're out of your mind because of the heat. And they will be looking at you. Remember, everybody is dying to see who talked Lincoln Monroe into marriage. Even considering everything I've heard about your Community and how the two of you met, it doesn't seem possible that he would have gone through the ceremony just because of some antiquated rules."

"He's a man of his word. I am honored to be his wife."

"He should be honored to be your husband."

"Don't tell Linc, but Bud is teaching me how to drive the truck."

"Why don't you want Linc to know?"

"I want to surprise him, too. I hope he'll be very impressed."

"I believe he's already impressed with you. He married you, didn't he?"

But not for long. Tempted to confide the truth of Linc's arrangement with her about the annulment, Rachel confined herself to her usual chatter instead.

Linda enjoyed talking about almost anything and loved to fuss over all things feminine. Rachel was glad of her guidance.

"Rachel, is Linc going to church with us tomorrow? I've never heard of him setting foot in one before."

"Goodness gracious. I've been so busy, I didn't ask him about church at all. I assumed he would want to attend."

"Don't make assumptions about Linc. He's liable to do the exact opposite of what you expect."

Linda's prediction turned out to be true. When nine o'clock Sunday morning dawned, what Linc objected to was not her desire to go to church. What he objected to was the cool little dress she and Linda had so painstakingly altered.

Ever since Linc had brought his wife home with him, he had been thinking about when and where he and Rachel would make their public debut as a couple. Because of the overwhelming interest his employees had shown when he had introduced Rachel to them, Linc suspected there would be plenty of rumors and speculation among the locals about how long and well she had known him before he brought her home as his wife.

To foil the gossips, he showed some affection towards her. The timetable for the annulment wouldn't be set until he took her to town. There would be less questions for him to field if he acted like they were a regular married couple for the time being.

He didn't want Rachel to have to field a bunch of

questions about their relationship, either. To suffer the humiliation of having to admit that she had been put up for auction and then married a man she had never set eyes on before was not something she should have to go through.

He decided it was important to launch a pre-emptive strike, however, when he heard she wanted to start attending services at the local church.

He hoped that an expensive engagement ring alongside Rachel's wedding band would announce to the world that they had indeed known each other long enough to *have* an engagement.

For the tenth time that morning he checked the placement of *his* wedding band. The ring felt tight on his finger, one of the reasons he hadn't worn it since Rachel had given it to him. He figured he should wear it today, though. Unfortunately, he also couldn't recall if the ring was supposed to go on his right hand or his left hand. Husbands were supposed to care about such trivial bits of information.

What Linc cared about were appearances and the conclusions his friends and neighbors might reach because of those appearances.

But Linc didn't think he cared one whit about her appearance until she came bounding down the stairs that morning, dressed in her Sunday best.

It was the same pale pink dress she had been wearing at the auction, he realized with a pang of recognition. The same dress she'd worn to their wedding. Only now it was a shadow of itself. The sleeves were gone. The hem had been raised to show Rachel's legs. Her very long and shapely legs.

On any other woman, the small dip in the neckline would have looked demure. Yet Rachel wasn't any other woman. Linc couldn't seem to take his eyes off the subtle hint of cleavage it revealed.

"Where do you think you're going?" he demanded.

"To church," she answered agreeably.

He caught himself before he fully lit into her. To criticize her appearance was to risk undermining her confidence. "Do you want me to give you a ride?"

"Only if you'd like to attend the services."

"The wide-open spaces are enough church for me."

"Big-sky country is the finest cathedral there is," she said.

Somehow he had hoped she would have become sanctimonious and argued the point with him. Then he would have reason to go with her in order to prove how open-minded he was. He didn't have an excuse to change his mind about going to church now.

The horn from a truck blasted outside. "That will be Bud and Linda," Rachel said. "They offered to take me. There's a picnic afterward. I'm not sure when you can expect me home."

"Wait," Linc said, catching her hand. Reaching into his shirt pocket, he slipped the filigreed diamond ring alongside the gold of her wedding band. "I want you to wear this from now on."

"Goodness gracious, it's beautiful. But whose is it?"

"Yours," he answered. "By way of my grandmother. Think of it as an engagement ring. In today's world, most married ladies wear one.''

To his satisfaction she held her hand up to the light, gazing at the faceted diamond in fascination. ''I have never worn anything so fine in all my life. Thank you for making me feel like I have a chance to fit in with all the people who are curious about me. I promise to return the ring the moment I come home today.''

''Keep it. It's wasted on a confirmed bachelor like me.''

''I can't do that.'' Her refusal was drowned by another horn blast.

''Listen, Rachel, if people ask you how long we've known each other, it wouldn't be a good idea to say we just met. It could be very embarrassing.''

''But, Linc, I couldn't lie.''

He sighed. ''No, Rachel, I guess you couldn't.''

''But I could say that I feel as if we've known each other forever,'' she said with a twinkle in her eye.

Linc smiled. ''Better get going or you'll be late.''

Rising on tiptoe, Rachel pecked Linc's cheek. ''Thank you for thinking of everything,'' she whispered.

He watched from the front porch with his hands in his pockets as Rachel climbed into the truck. Linc felt an overwhelming sense of déjà vu and, without wasting any more of his precious time, yanked on his roping gloves.

After two hours spent wrestling calves into the dust, he wiped the sweat from his brow and noticed Bud's truck driving into the yard.

Linc didn't even bother to wave. What he had to remember was that Rachel represented nothing more than another training project to him.

Six

Rachel nibbled at the eraser end of her pencil. She was still having trouble using the vast array of pens available in Linc's house for writing purposes. People of The Community used homemade pencils. She was getting used to the smooth yellow finish of machine-made pencils, but she hated using the pens.

First of all, she couldn't erase her mistakes. Second, the ink tended to make the so-called ballpoint tip slide across paper. The ink inevitably smeared, especially when she practiced writing pretend checks for pretend bills in order to learn how to manage her money. Linc had also taken on the responsibility of seeing that she understood the basic principles of electric power and other sources of energy. He was teaching her how to use the most commonly used machines, such as the computer and VCR, and started by showing her how to take photographs and make videos from a camera, though her efforts were unrecognizable when compared to those she saw in the magazines and on TV.

Meanwhile, Linda was introducing her to the kind of clothes regular people wore instead of the flashy costumes and fancy duds, as she called them, that Rachel had been studying in her quest to fit into the new world she had entered. They pored over catalogs and pictures from sewing patterns that Linda had used in making clothes for her two grown daughters.

After several days of planning what she wanted to buy, Rachel placed her first catalog order, buying her own sensible jeans, blouses, underwear and socks. Because she had yet to open her own checking account, Linc had her use his credit card. She then reimbursed him in cash for her clothes, paying out from her cache of one hundred dollar bills.

Linda showed her how to use more modern day conveniences, too, such as the vacuum cleaner and electric iron. Cleaning supplies were supposed to be modern, too. In Rachel's mind, however, what Linda called antibacterial agents and other detergents couldn't replace good old-fashioned vinegar and ammonia.

The laundry machines for washing and drying clothes were a whole different matter. She marveled at the froth of bubbles and the movement of the washer. And the dryer. What a boon in winter. No more frozen sheets on the clotheslines.

But learning how to manage a modern household

wasn't enough for her without Linc around. From the beginning she could tell he was a solitary man, given to long spans of time where he needed to be alone in order to refresh himself. She, too, needed refreshment and used prayer to do it. But Linc's solitude was by choice rather than an expression of his true nature.

In the past, she had made similar choices to remain alone, choices designed to protect herself from the hurt of rejection. As she watched Linc bury himself in constant work, work he believed only he could do, she wondered what hurts he had suffered. Perhaps it was none of her business. Soon she would be packed off to live in town. Besides, Linc had to come to terms with the past in his own way and in his own time. The auction had been her vehicle for release. She must have faith that he would find his vehicle as well.

She liked to study the weathered creases on his face, especially when he focused on a single task. Concentration was one of his special gifts, perseverance another. He used both wisely in his training of horses and the rich people who owned them.

She had noticed that Lincoln wasn't one to smile often. Yet at heart he was an unforbidding man, given to great kindness and generosity. His sense of humor was easily tickled, indicated by the twitching alongside his mouth. Subtlety suited him, for when he was really amused, the most amazing dimple appeared along his lean cheek.

He had a tendency to search the horizon as though looking for what yet couldn't be seen. In wondering what it was, Rachel felt an inevitable quivering in her stomach. He looked at her like that once before, on the day of the auction, making the hairs rise on the back of her neck. And when he asked her to marry him, his gaze finally rested on her, and she was overwhelmed by the feeling that she was what he had been searching for.

The feeling came back when he touched her, kissed her. That was why she'd been devastated after he let down her hair and led her to believe they would lay together on their wedding night. Despite her best efforts not to rely on the feeling any more, it was growing stronger. The past several weeks, she had learned so much, thanks to Linc.

But her time was running out. Inevitably he would insist on annulling the marriage, and inevitably she would agree. To argue would invite his contempt. Contempt for going back on her word. To Linc, there was no greater sin. The greatest sin for her would be to insist on staying where she wasn't wanted. Rather than commit the unpardonable, she would leave his ranch with her head held high.

Until that time, however, her longing for him would be difficult to hide. Indeed she wondered if she should hide it. Hiding was what her life had been all about when she lived in The Community, when she felt compelled to hide her skills in her effort to fit in. But here at Linc's ranch, her skills were appreciated, even necessary. Here, full of purpose, she felt her soul bursting from its bounds. She imagined the wonders of the world opening to her. The biggest wonder of all, of course, was Linc.

He had to be aware of the connection between them. Yet, if she offered to lay with him and he refused her again, she would feel worse devastation than she did before. Before, he had merely been her husband, someone she owed allegiance to. Now she owed him more. She owed him for his kindness in allowing her to stay here especially now that it was longer than originally agreed. She owed him for giving his precious attention and time to her without complaint, for letting Linda and Bud guide her and, last but not least, for letting the training of Summer be her reward.

Maybe there was no changing the inevitable. Maybe she was fooling herself to think her unpracticed, clumsy advances might be acceptable to Linc. She would try, however. As soon as she was able, she would try.

The following afternoon Rachel marched into Linc's office and waited until he narrowed his eyes at her. "Why don't you sit down, Rachel, and tell me what you need?"

She shook her head at his invitation to sit down in the leather chair opposite his desk and folded her arms instead. "For my remaining time here, I should like to have the use of a riding horse from your stables."

Linc leaned back in his chair. He should have thought of giving her her own horse to ride long before now. Training Summer was no longer as time-consuming as it once was. Linc had been wracking his brain trying to keep Rachel busy and out of trouble between lessons on local geography, map reading and finding her way around towns.

"No problem," he said. "Take your pick. Don't

worry about using my horses. You'll be doing me a favor by exercising them. Just make sure you let Bud know where you're going and when you plan to be home.''

He dismissed her by lowering his head and going back to his paperwork. Rather than leave with her tail between her legs, Rachel flattened her hand on the page of the book he was reading. ''Linc, I'd like you to go with me.''

''I don't have the time,'' he said without looking up. ''Ask Bud to go with you.''

''I don't want Bud. I want you.''

Linc noted her frank appraisal of him. The slightest of smiles touched her lips. If he didn't know better, he'd say Rachel was teasing him. ''I don't think you fully understand, Rachel. I have a business to run. There are phone calls to make, owners to see, horses that I'm training for world class events. Sorry, but I can't go with you.''

She shoved her hands in the back pockets of her jeans, obviously unwilling to take no for an answer. Because of the pull of her shirt across her chest, the full curves of her breasts pressed through. ''It's a beautiful leaf-growing day. I promise the ride will be short.''

Growing leaves. Just what he wanted to see. Linc scowled. What he really wanted to see was right in front of his face. Her nipples were hardening. He felt the stirring of arousal. ''How short?''

She cocked her hip but ruined the flirtatious effect by refolding her arms across her chest. ''Come with me and find out.''

Twenty minutes later, Linc was mounting his favorite gelding while Rachel was mounting his prized Paint mare. He still was ruminating about why he consented to take time away from work to ride with her. There was no way he was going to give into his attraction to her. It wasn't fair to lead her on in any way, shape, or form.

He muttered to himself that it was important to find out if she could handle her flashy mount. Gentling horses was well and good, but exercising highly trained cutting and reining horses might be beyond her capabilities. He also owed her the pleasure of his company when she so directly asked. It was the least he could do since she tried so hard to learn what he felt she should know.

Linc watched Rachel critically while she mounted smoothly with one quick hop from the ground. She adjusted the length of her stirrups while in the saddle, then glanced at him questionably.

"Where to?" she asked.

"I'll show you the pasture that has the most trails on it. We'll go out east of the ranch. If you want to stay out there for a while, it will be easy to find your way back."

He spurred his gelding into an easy lope and led the way to the east gate, halting to open it for Rachel, allowing her to pass through without dismounting.

Clearing the gate, she kicked her horse and galloped away. He spun his gelding and slammed the gate shut, but she was already a good hundred yards away. Charging after her, he worried that he had underestimated her ability to handle the Paint.

Her hair loosened from its mooring and streamed out like a flag above the brown and white patches on the Paint's powerful hindquarters. "Yi, yi, yi," she yelled, whooping like a wild Indian.

Flabbergasted to discover she was entirely in control of this mad, headlong dash, Linc spurred his horse to intercept her. Was she nuts? On an unfamiliar mount, on unfamiliar terrain, she was liable to kill herself. If she didn't, he would kill her for taking off like that and scaring him witless...if he ever caught up with her.

Ridden by a woman who weighed little more than one hundred pounds, the Paint stretched out in full flight, showing off her championship lines, running true as a rifle shot.

Stretched out in similar flight and leaning low across the gelding's neck, Linc gave his horse every advantage he could, cutting across Rachel's more circuitous path, saving strides here and there. He even threw his cowboy hat aside, letting it fall to the ground, reducing as much air resistance as possible.

Scrubby sage and buffalo grass rushed past, blurred by speed. The wind stung his slitted eyes, making them water. Wind and the adrenaline rush of wild flight stole his breath. He used to ride like this all the time, like a native of the plains, bent low over the whipping mane of his pony Junie's neck, breathing the smell of sage and baked earth, and feeling the hot Texas sun burn his bare back.

He yelped like he used to, war whoops high in his throat. "Yi, yi, yahoo!"

He heard Rachel's echoing yell from the distance

far ahead. Between them, the gap was widening. He refused to lose. Time to try an old Indian trick and scare her witless.

Rodeo event riding required learning to fall from a bucking bull or speeding bronc without getting injured. Part art, part science, Linc had saved himself from serious injury more than once by knowing how to do it and when to use it.

He picked a path along a line of thicker sagebrush, kicked his feet out of the stirrups and twisted left, pushing away from his horse in order to miss its flying hooves. He hit the ground curled in a ball and allowed momentum to take him, rolling over and over tufts of sagebrush, absorbing the shock of falling. The veteran rodeo performer in him made sure he kicked up plenty of dust before he rolled to a stop and stretched out, limp and lifeless.

It took less than thirty seconds for the pounding sound of hoofbeats to near. "Linc!"

Feeling guilty, he flicked his eyes open to see her jump to the ground and sink to her knees beside him. The look of sheer terror on her face made him blink as though he was just coming to.

"Linc, can you hear me?"

"I hear you," he grated, tasting grit. He figured he deserved it, but damn, it was worth seeing how concerned she was. Lord knew she had scared him half out of his mind too many times to count.

She ran her hands over his chest. "Are you all right?"

His eyes flickered closed while he took a minute to enjoy her attention. He'd missed touching her.

He'd missed being touched by her, too. "I'm all right," he murmured. "Got the wind knocked out of me, is all."

"Are you sure?"

All he was sure of was that he wanted the minute to go on forever. He coughed weakly. "Don't worry your pretty little head about me. I'm fine."

She huffed with doubt and laid the back of her hand against his forehead. "I can tell by the strain on your face that something is wrong. Where does it hurt?"

He clutched his stomach and doubled over on the ground. The last thing he needed was for her to notice a certain part of his anatomy straining against the button fly of his jeans.

She rolled him onto his back, pushed through his hands and unsnapped his shirt, ripping it open to reveal his chest. "You must have broken something." Renewed worry wrinkled her brow as she hovered over him, peering and gently pressing his abdominal region.

He groaned, giving voice to the overwhelming desire he felt.

"You have to tell me, Linc. Where does it hurt?"

"It's my heart," he whispered. "It's beating too fast."

Panicked, she put her ear to his chest. "Oh, please, Lord, no, not Linc's heart."

He felt immediate guilt and stroked her head to reassure her. "I'm okay, Rachel. Really. I fell off my horse on purpose. I was just joking around."

"Joking around?" She slowly sat up, looking absolutely stricken. "You were pretending? All this time you were making a *fool* of me?"

Too late he recalled how sensitive she was to that particular word. "Rachel, I'm sorry. You aren't the fool. I am. I was trying to scare you. It was a dumb thing for me to do."

"No, I'm the dumb one. I *believed* you."

"No, you're not dumb. I didn't mean it. Don't cry. Please, don't cry."

She wiped at the tears. They kept coming, though, coming from deep inside. Sobbing, she buried her face in her hands.

Linc circled his arms around her, cursing his thoughtlessness. "Shhh. I didn't mean to be cruel."

"It's not your fault. It's mine," she cried.

"How can it be your fault?"

She inhaled slowly, her expression taking on a distracted, faraway cast. "When I was a girl, the children at school made up a game. Fool the fool, they called it. They planned it ahead."

"Planned it?"

Rachel sighed. "Behind my back, they whispered about me. They called me names and did things, mean things. At first it was harmless pranks like tying my shoelaces together or offering to shake my hand with burrs in their palms. Then one day a boy in my grade came running into the schoolyard before the teacher was there, yelling that a little girl had fallen into the water well. When I ran to the well to help, he threw me in. He was lying, of course. I was so ashamed to be fooled like that, I skipped school for the rest of the year. Another time a boy poured pig's blood over his chest and pretended to be stabbed by a pocket knife. I tried to stop the blood, and he started laughing. Everybody laughed.''

Rage swept Linc, clenching his jaw and roughening his voice. "Where were your teachers when all this was going on?"

"The Community school has one classroom and one teacher. I didn't want to tattle. There is an old saying, 'Sticks and stones will break my bones, but names will never hurt me.' But after the pig's blood, I told her. She said such trials and tribulations would build my character."

Linc swore. "She should have stopped it, Rachel. What happened to you wasn't right."

"I know I shouldn't dwell on it. It happened long ago. I felt so alone, though. I showed them how I listened to horses and such. That was before I knew better than to tell anyone. They said I was odd and touched in the head."

"If I had been there, I would have decked anybody who said that. Didn't your parents do something?"

"Yes, they loved and comforted me. They said not to listen to the bad things, but dwell on the good things."

"I hate to say it, Rachel, but The Community is evil. I'm glad you got out of there."

"Granny Isaacs isn't evil. She stopped the shunning when she became an elder. She was always kind to me. So were others. Every situation has a good side and a bad side. In my loneliness, I turned to horses. I watched and rode and studied them. I learned how to listen better than I ever had before."

"That doesn't make what happened right." He reached for her hand, but she pulled away, straightening up and scrubbing at her face.

"My, what a tale," she said in a bravely wobbly voice. "You must be bored to tears."

"Rachel, you could never bore me. Come here. Let me hold you."

"No, thank you. I'm fine." Her smile was wobbly, too. But she threw back her shoulders and shook her finger at him in a scolding gesture. "Falling off your horse, pretending to be hurt—Lincoln Monroe, I ought to horsewhip you."

Knowing she was trying to salvage her pride, he matched the exaggerated note in her injured tone. "You ride like the wind. I had to catch you somehow. Am I forgiven?"

"No, you're not forgiven." She put her hands on her hips and scooted closer to him. "You have to kiss me first."

"Kiss you? Where? Here?" He teased her lips, rimming them with the merest edge of his thumb. She shivered wildly. He chuckled and lightly pinched her nose. "Or here?"

Her hands went to the top button of her blouse and quickly went down the front. "Everywhere."

His grin faded. "Rachel, you don't know what you're asking."

"Yes, I do. You think I am some errant person who doesn't know her own mind. But I know what I want, what I love. I love it here, on your ranch. I am falling in love with you."

Her declaration thickened his throat and remorse at

the silence hanging between them filled him. He knew what he wanted, too. Love was last on his list. There was too much to do in this life, too much he wanted to accomplish with his training business and his ranch. Yet to hurt Rachel with the truth...Linc refused to do it. He also refused to lie to her, too. "Rachel, there is so much beyond this valley, so much that you haven't experienced. There's plenty of good men out there. You could do so much better than me. You're bright, ambitious, gifted. Give yourself some time to find your own place in the world."

"I have a place here with you."

He scooped a handful of hair and tucked it behind her ear, then fingered her mutinous jaw. "It's not that I don't want to make love with you. I think about it all the time. But I worry that someday you will regret it."

"I won't."

More than his heart was pounding now. Every nerve, every fiber of his being strained toward her. Rarely did he turn down a sure thing. But he had to this time. She was too precious, too special to have her first sexual experience be with a man who didn't love her. If she needed a shoulder to cry on, he would find some way to put aside this throbbing desire and be there for her, come hell or high water—for now. But that was it. "I'll hold you, okay?"

He rolled from his sitting position and crawled to her on his hands and knees, trying to make her laugh or smile at least, to release the tension between them. It didn't happen. She did, however, roll to her knees and walk forward on them to meet him.

She halted a few inches away, her gaze provocative. Unsure as to why, he straightened and brushed back her hair. Her hand grazed the bulge fronting his jeans. "May I see?"

His voice came out as though he were strangling. "What a question. No."

"I'm curious. I'm here to learn."

He pushed away her hand. "I bet you are. You're like a little cat, way too curious for your own good."

She gave him a puzzled frown. "I like it when you touch me. Won't you like it if I touch you?"

His body was responding as though she were touching him. Sweat broke out on his forehead. "That's not the point, Rachel."

"But you said you would teach me all there is to know about living in your world."

"That was before I found out what exactly you wanted to know."

"Linc, I am nearly thirty years old. If I should marry again, I'm afraid I'll be shamed by my own ignorance."

The day of their marriage, he had been cynical enough to suspect she may have had ulterior motives, that she was using every feminine wile to trap him into giving her what she wanted—marriage till death us do part. But Rachel was guileless, without a dishonest bone in her body. Whatever she did, she did out of instinct. But that didn't awaken his instinct to settle down. Instinct instead told him to find a way to respond to her without making her his own. What if she had her first experience with a man who didn't appreciate her? There were so many jerks out there.

After the story she'd told him, Linc recognized as never before how vulnerable Rachel was to mind games and manipulation. If he didn't teach her what to expect, who would? Some cretin off the street?

Linc shuddered at the thought. He shuddered again, inside and out. The possibility of making love to her hit him hard. The perfection of the day, crystalline air, a bed of emerald grass. Here they were, just the two of them, in the middle of the prettiest meadow he owned.

A light breeze stirred her hair, bringing the fragrance of sage and pine. He couldn't have picked a better place if he tried. Rachel belonged in the sun. She belonged to the sky.

He began with a kiss on her forehead. She welcomed him with open arms. He plundered her then, no longer capable of holding back.

Giddiness filled Rachel. Victorious giddiness, feminine giddiness. He crushed her to him, the muscles of his arms like bands of iron. She couldn't breathe and didn't care. His powerful thighs were equally hard, as hard as the bulge that fit the natural hollow at the apex of her thighs.

She gasped as fever liquefied her body. He rocked against her, huge and hard, lifting her to ride him, to rub him. The most natural of urges had her spreading her legs.

He groaned and gripped her bottom, holding her tight as he laid her down on the cool grass. Supporting himself with his arms, both locked on either side of her, he loomed above her. "Can you feel what you do to me?"

"Can you feel what you do to me?" she asked.

Linc sat back on his haunches and threw off his shirt, whipped off his belt. The sun made his eyes glitter like gems as he started on the button fly of his jeans. Rachel held her breath at the sight of widening denim and the snowy cotton underneath.

With his jeans still on, he leaned over her. "Rachel, are you sure you want to do this? Tell me the truth."

"Yes," she whispered. "Yes."

He began unbuttoning her blouse. "I don't want to shock you. We're going to go real slow."

He laid open her blouse and slid his hands behind her back, elevating her enough to get her arms out of her sleeves. Blunt fingers unhooked the back of her bra. He removed that, too, tossing it aside. After arranging her blouse like a blanket beneath her, he eased her back down on the grass.

She smelled the earth and the prickling of tiny grass blades through her blouse. The sun warmed her chest, but it was Linc's scrutiny that fired the familiar aching within her breasts. "Just looking at you makes me hot," he said. "I've tasted your golden skin and your softness and all I want to do is bury myself inside you."

He laid his hands upon her and kneaded the tender flesh. "I'm going to kiss you everywhere, just like you asked. I'll make you hot, as hot and swollen as I am. And I promise, promise from the bottom of my heart, that nothing will hurt. You will only feel good. Extremely good."

He raked his fingernails lightly from breast to breast. She arched her spine upward, gasping as he rolled her nipples between his forefingers and thumbs. "I already feel good," she whispered hoarsely.

He tugged and played with the tips of her breasts and, greedy for more, she arched higher and higher, seeking a pleasure such as she had never known. He obliged with his tongue, suckling her into ecstasy. "Would you believe it gets better than this?"

She turned her head from side to side, frantically panting and clenching her fists. "How...?" she asked, dragging the syllable out.

"Here's how." He blew on the moisture he had laved on her skin. Air rushed from her lungs. Groping, she found his chest and clung to him.

"I feel too good," she cried.

"Shhh, relax. We're not done yet."

She opened dazed eyes. "We're not?"

He eased down on the grass next to her. She noticed he winced, adjusting the fit of his wide-open jeans. "I think we may be moving a mite too fast. Let's take a rest."

She felt too restless to rest. "What about you? You need to feel good, too."

He stretched out on his side and propped his head on his hand. "I did."

"Did?"

"I haven't lost control like that since I was a teenager. Watching you was all it took. And we still have plenty to do, plenty to try."

Confused, she grazed the opening of his jeans and encountered astounding heat and moisture. He crooked a smile.

"See? I did good," he said.

Rachel cupped the heat, feeling how relaxed he had become.

His expression was relaxed, too. "I know I've never done this before," she said, "but don't we have to take the rest of our clothes off?"

"You first. I'll explain why later."

If he wanted her to go first, Rachel realized he must truly like to watch her. Fighting shyness, she wiggled her hips and shimmied from her jeans, dragging down her underpants, too.

Linc reached for his discarded shirt and spread it underneath her. He lifted his head and his gaze drifted downward. She felt as if she were blushing all over. The best cure for self-consciousness, she thought, was to become very conscious of somebody else.

She gazed at him, noting the flat male nipples barely visible beneath his chest hair. Curious, she traced a circle around the nearest one. There was an immediate reaction. Every one of his chest and arm muscles flexed. His face didn't look nearly as relaxed now.

She rolled the tiny knot between her forefinger and thumb and searched for the other, lightly raking him with her fingernails. Once she found what she was looking for, she kissed and licked, surprised by his sweet, salty taste.

He whispered her name. "Rachel, where in the heck did you learn to do that?"

Giggling, she blew on the moisture she'd left on his chest. "I was taught by a master."

"He's not done with you, either. Give me one of your feet. I intend to kiss you all over."

She gave him one of her feet. Palming her heel, he stroked his way up and down the length of her legs, massaging her feet and calves, exploring her dimpled knees and circling her thighs.

Fever spread like wildfire under her skin. She was vaguely aware of the silky slide of his hands up and over her hips, then the brush of fingers in her silky curls. "Lincoln?"

"Relax, Rachel. Nothing bad is going to happen. I promise." He covered her with his wide hand, and she widened her eyes at the intense sensation that snaked through her.

"Do you like that?"

"Yes. Oh, yes."

"If you want, let yourself move. Press your body against my hand. Does it feel good?"

Rachel couldn't find a way to speak. Her hips moved of their own accord, rocking and searching—for what she didn't know. But Linc seemed to know. He shifted to lie beside her, handling her with patience and care, his fingers stroking. The sensations spiraled, and she shivered on the crest of a soaring pleasure.

"Let yourself feel the strength of it, Rachel. Let yourself go."

She clutched his arm, his shoulder, digging her nails in at the rhythmic waves crashing through her. Calling Linc's name, she came back to earth, totally spent but alive.

"You're beautiful, Rachel, you know that?"

She smiled in gratitude, awed by the ecstasy Linc had given her. He brushed his lips across her forehead, but instead of withdrawing his fingers, he stroked her again, featherlight and sure of what he was about. The onslaught of sensation spiraled quickly, then he paused.

"See how responsive you are? As warm, moist and sweet as a meadow flower." He opened her in an indescribable way that caused her to shiver over and over again. But the worst part was that she wanted to make him shiver, too.

She encountered the open vee of his jeans and the softer material of his underwear. She cupped him as he cupped her and felt his kiss brush her lips. "I wish it could happen again for me like it can for you."

"Why can't it happen for you?" she murmured, rubbing him gently yet firmly, marveling at the thickening she felt within her palm. In his own way he was just as beautiful as he claimed she was.

He dragged in a long breath. "What are you doing to me?" he asked.

"The same thing you're doing to me?" she answered, smiling into his eyes. His body hardened precipitously.

"I'll be damned."

"No, you won't be damned—not if I can help it. What else can I do to make you feel good?"

"I don't suppose you have a little foil packet in your wallet, do you?"

"Foil packet?"

"Never mind," he said and renewed his gentle stroking of her. "It's not important."

Rachel was finding it difficult to maintain her train of thought. "Wait a minute. What's not impor—"

She pushed his hand away and sat up. She put her hands to her burning cheeks. "Oh, my. Oh, Linc. I didn't want it to come out this way. I should have told you at the beginning, but I was so swept up by how good you make me feel, I completely forgot. I should have told you when Linda and I first went to the clinic, but I was embarrassed and I wasn't sure how to bring my decision up—"

"Whoa, honey. Slow down. I don't have a clue what you're talking about."

"I'm talking about what's inside those foil packets," she whispered. "It's a method of birth control."

"You know about birth control?" Now he sounded breathless.

"Yes. Linda and I went to a health clinic. She needed to have a physical. She thought I should have one, too. The doctor asked if I was married and when I said yes, she showed me the different methods of birth control. I decided on The Pill."

"You decided on The Pill?"

"Oh, dear. I knew I should have consulted with you."

"You're on The Pill. Is that what you're telling me?"

"For more than a month now. Linda took me to the clinic the first week I came here."

Linc kissed her and rubbed her nose in an affectionate gesture. "Rachel, you amaze me more and more every day. Do you know that?"

"You amaze me, Linc. The way you kiss..." she stared at his mouth.

Chuckling, he kissed her again, cherishing her with

his mouth, his caress. She sank against him and he held her tight, kissing her until she moaned in quick little breaths. He secreted his hand between her thighs and she opened them, allowing his fingers to discover how she was quivering within, ready to burst.

"No, wait," she gasped. "It's your turn." She tugged at his jeans and underwear, pushing them off.

Unconfined by his clothes, his sex more than filled her hand, the tautness shivering against her, shivering as she had wanted him to shiver. "How about it's both our turns?" he said, his voice catching between breaths. "We'll make it happen at the same time."

"Goodness gracious," she whispered. "Is that possible?"

"I'm beginning to think anything is possible with you."

He kissed her, cupped and stroked her. Rocking against his hand, she called out his name in ecstasy. He shifted his weight and positioned his body as though seeking the center of that ecstasy. Sensation slowly slid through her. Just thinking about his tenderness brought her to the point of being overwhelmed. With every sensuous wave came a sense that Linc was filling her with heat. Finally their hips locked together as their gazes locked together, vivid blue versus turbulent green.

They rocked together as one. His every muscle tensed. Stretched into total release, Rachel moaned low in her throat. The vibration swept through both of them, spasms that melted flesh into pure feeling.

Suspended by pleasure, they stayed that way for many minutes.

Linc eased out of her as slowly as he had eased himself in, progressing in minute increments, wincing at the thought of hurting her in any way. He studied her expression, anticipating the tiniest indication of pain. Except her lips curled upward at the corners, much as her eyes did, slumberous and sated.

The fresh scent of crushed grass took him back, back to the day he met her. It seemed long ago rather than mere weeks. He recalled her nervous apprehension when he'd clasped her hand then, and the unreality that had hovered over the entire scene of their symbolic joining.

Today was the real thing.

Restlessly shifting his weight, Linc rolled onto his back, drawing Rachel with him and nestling her head in his shoulder. She sighed in contentment, and he felt the urge to do so, too, but the memory of their first conversation and the subsequent wedding vows nagged at his conscience. He'd informed her the marriage would be annulled, sure, but he had also made promises to her, promises to protect and care for her, like any groom did to his bride. He was the one who made her feel like his wife. No wonder she hoped the marriage would continue. Worse, he was still making promises to her, promises sealed with kisses and mind-blowing sex.

He stroked her hair, reminding himself that she was an adult, fully capable of making decisions for herself. Hell, the proof was in the way she had taken the bull by the horns with the issue of birth control. Sleeping together didn't have to be the big deal he once thought it was. She wanted him as much as he wanted her.

Nope, he thought. Nobody had ever desired, ever fantasized, ever obsessed the way he desired, fantasized and obsessed about her.

Would he ever tire of her? Right now, he didn't think it was possible. He didn't think it was possible he could lose faith in her, either.

He would, though. He always did.

Long before he grew to manhood, he found it difficult to show the least bit of interest in the things most women found important. He cared about his mother, though, and pretended to feel differently, forcing himself to listen to her prattle on about all sorts of nonsense. He'd learned how to cook at her elbow. His real enjoyment of it didn't come until he'd grown competent enough to take over the job from her when he was nine. She didn't mind. She seemed grateful to have more time to talk on the phone and left home soon after.

As he got older, girls his age or above did have the power to fascinate him. He still found it difficult to relate to most of their concerns, but he certainly reaped the benefits of pretending otherwise. His first real girlfriend said he had the eyes of a tiger and the soul of the most sensitive and fragile of birds.

At seventeen, he dropped out of high school and joined the rodeo circuit full time. His girlfriend cried so much at his leaving, he broke up with her.

With traveling by day and performing at night, he found the cowgirls on the circuit to be his best bet when it came to the opposite sex. He also thought that with all he had in common with them, finding one to spend some quality time with would be a cinch. But even with the same interests he couldn't seem to find common ground.

When he finally did, she was a twenty-four-year-old barrel racer. In short, she broke his heart. But not without playing with it for a good long time.

His biggest regret was that he hadn't seen it coming. She was the one who left the relationship first, rather than the other way around.

He broke the next girlfriend's heart and the next before he came to his senses and realized the hurt he was causing. After that, he played the one-night-stand game with the one-night-stand girls. He was a bona fide rodeo star by then. It was hard to tell who was more impressed by his championship titles—the women who now flocked to him, but previously wouldn't have given him the time of day, or the shysters who wanted to trade on his money and his fame.

He might be retired now but little about him had changed. Rachel was his next, best example. Eventually, he would do something that hurt her—deliberate or inadvertent, it didn't matter. Resentment would fester. Distrust would grow. And the cycle would repeat itself, over and over, until there was nothing but hurt and blame and in the end, disgust on his part for allowing the relationship to become that serious in the first place.

But the self-loathing had already started, Linc realized. He had promised to free Rachel. Instead he had tied her more firmly to him than ever by making love. What in the world had he been thinking of?

He slipped his arm out from under her head. She smiled at him sleepily and stretched like a cat, revealing her relaxed ease. The urge to press himself against her and share that ease flowed through him like the warmth of the sun on his back, inexorable and impossible to control.

He caressed her, drinking in the sight, imprinting the curves and hollows in his memory. This would be the last time they made love, he promised himself. The only time.

He let her hold his hand after they dressed and he boosted her into the saddle. They rode back to the ranch at a slow walk, stealing glances. At some point, Linc felt his insides begin to close up, to shrink, and the closer they rode toward civilization, the more his silence expanded until it became louder than any words he could think of to say.

Once they reached the main yard, he tossed his reins to Bud and told Rachel he had work to do. She offered her help. He didn't need her help, he said. He didn't need anyone or anything.

He knew he sounded harsh. It was better than starting a fight, though. A fight where he might say worse things to her, casting blame where he shouldn't, as if she had somehow trapped him and he didn't want her around anymore.

Later that afternoon, after he'd done every possible chore and gone through all the paperwork in his office, Linc crossed the yard to check on the stock penned in the near pasture. He glimpsed Rachel sitting on the porch of the house in the sunlight, rocking in one of the rockers, her hair streaming over one shoulder like white water tumbling down. He knew in his gut that she'd spotted him. He ignored her though, grateful he couldn't see her eyes. Lying to her in the face of such clear blue would be like deliberately polluting an alpine lake.

Yet he would lie to her so as not to prolong her agony, lie by pretending nothing had changed between them. If she questioned him, he would become very matter-of-fact. She had learned how to make love, he would tell her. Now she had the experience to decide for herself whether or not she wanted to invite a man to her bed. It was another life lesson, providing her with the experience necessary to make an informed decision. No need to repeat it or review it, he would say. She had passed with flying colors.

Though they were now married in every sense of the word, Linc didn't change one iota of his evening routine. As he did every night, he started making supper as the setting sun cast long shadows across the barnyard and corrals.

Thinking he would let her help because they had finally become one, Rachel washed her hands in the kitchen and set out to peel the carrots he'd laid out by the sink.

"What a lovely day it was," she commented, hoping that he would make some similar comment.

"Rachel, what are you doing?" he asked, firmly removing the carrot and scraper from her hands. "Making the meals is my job."

"I thought you could use some help."

He nudged her away from the sink as he had several times in the past when she had tried to help. "Working alone in the kitchen helps me relax, remember? This is also your time to find whatever it is you like to do after a long day."

How could she argue when she had already learned to respect his need to have this time to himself when he prepared the meals? "I do have some sewing I was hoping to finish up tonight."

"Good. Now, shoo. Supper will be ready in twenty minutes."

Later that evening they spent their usual hour together reading quietly in the great room. Rachel stared unseeingly at her open book, wondering when she should broach the subject of their lying together again as husband and wife. When she finally gathered her courage and boldly asked which bed they would be retiring to that night, Linc said he would like to sleep alone in his own room. There was nothing angry, cutting or clever about the way he said it, either. It was a simple statement of fact.

Perhaps she should have pushed the issue that night because the next morning Linc acted no differently. He had previously scheduled a couple of hours to work together with her on the more advanced training of Summer. He showed up at the appointed hour and in his usual businesslike manner helped Rachel put the filly through her paces.

Afraid of broaching the subject that burned in her heart for fear he would tell her it was all a mistake, Rachel worked her fingers to the bone in the hopes that Linc would see her distress and relieve her misery by giving her more than a kind word or two. She

couldn't say he treated her badly or with indifference.
He exchanged the usual pleasantries and answered the
questions she had about contemporary life just as he
always did, with patience and humor.

Another day went by and another. Their time together was dwindling away. With a heavy heart Rachel realized Linc wasn't going to change his attitude
toward her. He didn't cancel their planned trip to
town next week to look at places for her to live. He
also informed her the annulment papers would be
picked up at the county courthouse, ready for the two
of them to sign.

To her old way of thinking, she might have felt as
though she were neglecting her duty to him. As the
end of the week came round, however, she decided
she would cooperate with his plans as best she could
because she loved him. If she couldn't believe he was
doing his best by her, then there wasn't much hope
for them, anyway.

Seven

The next day at dawn, or more accurately *before* dawn, Linc beat Rachel downstairs. Perhaps that wasn't such a bad thing, she decided. Despite weeks of practice, she was still struggling with her cooking skills. His biscuits were large, fluffy and golden brown, his bacon crisp, his coffee dark brown and delicious.

"You're spoiling me," she said over breakfast.

"There's a reason," Linc replied evenly, armored against anything she might do or say to alter his decision to finish up her education and get her the hell away from him. "We're going to town this morning," Linc stated succinctly. "Bring your money."

"I see," she said, her tone matching the measured sound of his. "What am I to buy?"

"A savings account, for one thing. Have you ever been to a bank before?"

"No. I'm not sure what it is."

"A bank is a safe place where no one can touch your money except you. You'll learn how one works. I also have supplies to pick up." He decided to save the news about visiting the county courthouse to have the annulment papers signed and filed until the last minute. He didn't need another argument. "We'll take a look around town and see what apartments are available. You need to find a place to live before you move out on your own."

"When will we return to the ranch?"

"Depends on how fast you learn."

"Then I shall learn quickly indeed."

Even hearing that, Linc had to admit Rachel was taking the trip to the town of Tall Timbers pretty damn well.

She hummed along with the country music songs on the radio during the two hours it took to drive the required 140 miles. He couldn't help but notice that she had obviously dressed with care. Her red-checked gingham blouse was new, and she had belted her denim jeans with silver studded leather. She had put up her hair, French braiding it tightly to the back of her head. Linda was apparently teaching her well. Rachel had also learned the magic of hair spray. Despite the truck's rolled-down windows, only a few tendrils teased her forehead as they sped along the highway.

As she hummed she casually put her right hand out the passenger window, riding the currents of air rushing past.

That memorable horseback ride he had taken with her immediately sprang to Linc's mind. Rachel had started the chase with her sudden flight across the prairie. But it was the wild gallop and the wind in his face that had given him such a sense of speed and exhilaration. He had felt free. Free to live as he used to—literally by the seat of his pants—free to let off steam and yell like a crazy man, free to have laughs and have fun. It was that sense of freedom that allowed him to feel free enough to simply lose his head with Rachel. Fooling her like that with a tricky fall. Then came his real fall from grace, treating her to what amounted to a quick roll in the hay and taking a gift from her that should never have belonged to him at all.

After they went to the bank, he broached the subject of the annulment papers. She turned sharply away from him, and he had to grab her hand to stop her from going who knew where. The only way he could get her to go back to the truck with him was to promise he wouldn't bring up the subject again that day. Bad idea. Her refusal to sign them left him in a sour mood. Short of twisting her arm, he would probably have to wait until she made the move to town. Maybe that was why he decided he needed a nice, stiff drink. And if she insisted on staying with him and being his damned shadow, then she would just have to come along and suffer in silence.

The bar held a Thursday afternoon crowd. Since he had to drive, he held himself to one beer. To get away from Rachel, Linc headed over to the pool tables. It was short work to get into a friendly game.

Once the place started filling up, though, more patrons wanted to play. Couples teamed up. It occurred to him that Rachel could use a nice little lesson in playing pool. It was one of those life skills that was needed to survive in the cold, cruel world in this part of Montana, at least.

He enjoyed bending over her to show her how to use the pool cue and hit the balls. She couldn't fight with him in front of all these people no matter how angry she might be with him.

She was awful at the game. She didn't seem to mind, though. Blue chalk smeared her chin. Instead of the game becoming intensely competitive, a camaraderie built around the table. It was the type of camaraderie that was infectious, and much as he didn't want it to infect him, it did, reminding him of his early days in rodeo when all the rookies hung out together, nursing the day's bumps and bruises, pooling their money to keep an occasional motel roof over their heads while commiserating to keep their lives and limbs together. He must be more hard up for company than he believed. Being one-on-one with Rachel must be driving him to distraction if he was having fun hanging out with the pool table crowd.

Rachel noticed how Linc's tense watchfulness with her relaxed as late afternoon slipped into evening. Here in the tavern he didn't have to play the part of the boss. He didn't have to be utterly focused on seeing to her education, either. He was just one of the guys, as he called it. Except for the ring on his finger.

''How long have you and your husband been married?'' asked one of the women they were playing with, a woman named Mary Lou. Rachel wasn't quite sure what to say. Her pretty, auburn hair styled in soft curls, Mary Lou had an open, freckled face and a perpetual expression of curiosity. She wore the clothes of what Rachel was coming to see as the working cowgirl. Mary Lou's checked shirt was tied at the waist and rolled up at the sleeves. Her blue jeans hugged her trim hips and long legs.

"Linc and I have been married for a short time," Rachel answered. "This is our first trip to town."

"I thought so," answered Mary Lou. "I haven't seen you around before and I know *everybody*. Even heard rumors about Linc Monroe buying up the old Ickes Ranch, though I'd never seen him. Everybody knows of him, though, what with his record number of all-around rodeo titles." Mary Lou fluffed her hair. "Makes me wish I had had a chance at him myself when he was still single."

Rachel wondered if Mary Lou soon would have that chance. She had that confident appearance that said quite clearly she belonged in this world. To see Linc through another woman's eyes left Rachel with the sinking feeling that she still had a long way to go when it came to belonging as Mary Lou did.

Excusing herself, Rachel headed for the ladies' room. Studying her appearance in the mirror, she pulled out her shirttails and knotted them at the waist. There was little she could do about her borrowed jeans, but she did undo the braid that held her hair and fluffed the long waves that fell around her face.

Feeling braver, she even unbuttoned the top two buttons on her blouse. If she'd been wearing her chemise, it would have shown, but her new brassiere didn't.

Throwing her shoulders back for courage, she exited and saw that Linc's turn to shoot had come up. Picking up her pool cue, she approached the table. His gaze flickered, noting her arrival. He abruptly straightened. "What did you do with your hair?"

It seemed an odd question to Rachel since the answer was obvious. "Our friends are waiting for you to shoot the ball."

"Looking *very* good, Rachel." Mary Lou's boyfriend, Sam, winked at her.

Rachel winked back, deciding that this must be a custom that added to the sincerity of his compliment. His smile certainly widened. "Thank you, Sam."

Linc threw his pool cue on the table. "Time to go," he said, and took Rachel's elbow in an unusually powerful grip.

Startled by the change in his manner, Rachel balked. "But I am enjoying myself so. Can't we stay?"

He stopped, dragged his hand through his hair in exasperation, then nodded. "Sure. If you're ready for your next lesson." He offered his beer to her, then wrapped her hand around the bottle. "Cheers." Linc kept his gaze on her as she tipped his bottle back. She sipped cautiously and started coughing, holding her throat. Instantly Linc was standing at her side, patting her back. "Are you all right?"

"Fine," she said, choking, trying not to draw any more attention to herself than she already had. "May we sit down?"

"Yeah." He grabbed her hand and led her to a table for two. "I'm sorry. I should have warned you."

"You won't always be here to warn me. I must experience these things on my own." She took another cautious sip. Knowing what to expect this time allowed her to better identify the mix of flavors. Barley, malt and the strange-tasting fizz. But the brew wasn't nearly as bitter as she first thought. "It's rather tasty," she admitted. "I like it."

"Don't like it too much."

"Why not?"

"Alcohol can make you do foolish things."

"Alcohol?"

"Sorry. Spirits, liquor." Oddly solicitous, he covered her hand. "What do you think of this place?"

"I like it," Rachel said as she downed her beer and requested another. "And the people are friendly."

"Being in a honky-tonk bar is not like a church social, Rachel. You don't have to introduce yourself to everyone you meet or say goodbye to them, either."

"Isn't that the polite thing to do?"

"Save the politeness for other places. Bars are not the safest places to meet people. Remember I told you how important it is to be on your guard?"

She glanced at him, and he recognized the glint of mutiny silvering her eyes even in the darkness of the bar. "It is tiring to be on guard all the time. Besides, I thought it would be good to be friendly in a place where the people are friendly in return. I wonder what it would be like to work here?"

Linc blanched, then figured that was the beer talking. Still, there was no harm in making his opinion known. "Trouble with a capital *T* is all you'll find in a job at a honky-tonk bar."

"But I wish to have a job where I can work with other people as a team, like your team of Clydesdales work together to pull a wagon. The cooks, waitresses and bartenders are very good at working together. Linc, I'm rather like a lead mare, I'm afraid. I need other horses around to feel useful."

"Does everything always come back to horses with you?"

"When I was little, I used to wish I was a horse. But today proves there are advantages to being human. Much as I like horses, they can't play pool."

"How about one last game of pool before we head out the door?" Linc asked two hours and four beers between them later. "I'd like to get home at a decent hour."

Rachel jumped from her bar stool and faced him, standing stiffly at attention, her arm cocked in a crisp military salute.

"Yes, sir, Mr. Lincoln, Sarge, sir," she said in the twang that made Jim Nabors famous.

"You've been watching too many Gomer Pyle reruns on television."

"I thought you *wanted* me to watch too much tel-abision."

Linc's gaze arrowed in on Rachel's face, noting her overbright eyes, happy smile and flushed complexion.

"Tell me, Rachel. How do you feel?"

She was thoughtful for a very long time, which confirmed his worst suspicions. "I feel like dancing," she finally replied.

Her legs tangled, and she grabbed for the stool. Linc righted her with a firm hand on her elbow and set her beer bottle on the bar. "I think you've had enough to drink tonight."

"You should slip some of that beer to the stallion of yours, Linc. I'm sure it would calm him directly."

Linc grabbed her coat, slung it over his arm and slipped the other arm around Rachel's waist. "Think so?"

"I know so," she announced in a loud tone more suitable for an annual pig-calling contest than anywhere else.

"Are you sure you don't feel sick?"

She peered at him, waving distractedly at the cigarette haze. "'Course not. We must be dancin', though. The room is spinning around."

He steered her to the door. "You've had too many beers. From now on remember that one bottle is enough for you."

"You had plenty more than me," she groused.

"I weigh more than you. Generally, that means the same amount of alcohol won't affect me like it would you. Plus I'm used to having a few beers. You're not."

"You mean if I have another beer I will get used to it?" she asked hopefully.

"No, that's not what I mean. Just take my word that one beer is your limit. Come on. I'm driving you home."

She broke away from him, her eyes wide and panicked. "But you've been drinking, too. Haven't you seen that TV commercial? 'A buddy doesn't let a buddy drive drunk.' Give me the keys."

"You've definitely been watching too much television."

She waited with her hand out. "Give me those keys, Lincoln Monroe. You and I are buddies."

Linc struggled to keep a straight face. She would hate to have him laugh at her. But he had to admit that despite her inebriated state, Rachel did have a point. He'd stopped drinking more than an hour ago in order to be able to drive home safely, but he needed another hour to get the alcohol out of his system. He'd been counting on spending some more time playing pool before they went home. He needed to find a place for him and Rachel to hang out for a while.

Unfortunately, Tall Timbers didn't exactly have much of a night life. The single movie theater closed its doors before ten p.m. Ellie's Café stayed open until nine for what the town considered its late diners, Linc knew, but it was way past that. There was a light on at the sheriff's office. Linc was certain he didn't want to go there, not with his tipsy wife. He supposed he and Rachel could sit on a bench outside the boarded-up windows of the old hardware store, but the wind was kicking up.

Tall Timbers did have two motels. Both did their best business in hunting season, which it wasn't. There shouldn't be any problem getting a couple of rooms for the night.

Towing Rachel, Linc headed for the most well-kept vacancy sign. The office was locked, but there was a note to ring the doorbell if help was needed.

The beer-bellied proprietor, dressed in a cowboy hat and a T-shirt covered by a plaid flannel robe, answered their call. "Hey," he said, his jowly face breaking out in a grin. "I know you. You're Lincoln Monroe. I seen your picture in all the horse and rodeo magazines."

There were times Lincoln resented being recognized all the time. If it helped him get waited on quicker tonight, though, he wasn't going to mind. "Hey, there," he said pleasantly. "I'd like a couple of rooms, please."

"Sure thing." The proprietor's attention shifted to Rachel. "Now this must be the missus. Heard tell she was a pretty little thing. Guess you'd agree with me that I heard right."

"I'm drunk," blurted Rachel.

"Howdy, Mrs. Monroe," the proprietor answered, ignoring her outburst and extending his hand with great respect. "It's a pleasure to meet you and Mr. Monroe."

Linc interrupted. "About those rooms?"

"You want two rooms, you say? That really ain't necessary, son. I got the biggest king bed in town. It's in my honeymoon suite. Only the best for our newlyweds."

"The honeymoon suite?" Linc asked, racking his brain for a good reason to insist on trading it for two smaller rooms. "How much a night is that?"

"On the house, son. On the house."

Linc pulled out his wallet. "I can't let you do that. Lincoln Monroe pays his own way."

"Not in your new hometown, you don't. Tall Timbers is honored to consider you a native son."

"Still like to pay my own way, if you don't mind."

"Heard tell you're originally from Texas. Aren't Texans known for their hospitality? You can't blame us Montanans for wanting to catch up."

"A-men," Rachel said.

Linc didn't know if he should chuckle or groan. Instead of doing either, he grabbed the graciously offered room key. "Appreciate it," he muttered.

The proprietor winked. "Anytime. By the way, feel free to use that suite past our usual checkout time if you feel the need."

Linc rolled his eyes heavenward. "Right."

Eight

"**R**achel, I need to take your boots off. Give me your feet."

Laid out on the king-size bed, Rachel rose up on her elbows and squinted. "Remember the last time I gave you my feet?"

Linc's head whipped up.

Her gaze zeroed in on the front of his jeans. "Yup, I can see you do remember." She flopped back on the bed, smiling beatifically. "It felt heavenly, Linc."

"Good Lord, Rachel. Be quiet and hold still."

"How many times do I have to tell you?" she scolded. "Don't take the Lord's name in vain. He'll send you to hell for sure."

Linc decided he already was in hell. Honeymoon-suite hell. The place where brides traditionally lost their virginity. The place where Rachel should have lost hers.

He yanked off her boots. "You need to get some sleep."

Rachel rolled off the bed. "I don't feel like sleeping." Raising her arms, she waltzed around the room and sashayed around the furniture.

He blocked her fall against the chair. "Be careful."

She wreathed his neck with her arms. "You make me dizzy, Lincoln Monroe. Did you know that?"

He did know it. He wished he didn't, though. He wished he didn't know that if he kissed her, she would give herself to him as naturally as a flower opened to the sun. "It's the beer that's making you dizzy. You need to lie down and sleep it off."

"Okay," she said agreeably. It had to be the first time she ever cooperated with him on the first try. Yet her easy compliance worsened the desire drumming along his veins. She smiled dreamily at him and flopped on the bed, forgetting that her arms still wreathed his neck.

Her weight shouldn't have flattened him like a left hook to the jaw. It did. The mattress bounced at their fall, springs singing. Her giggle mimicked the high, twangy sound.

He chuckled, too, and felt the rumbling of his chest shake his resolve to avoid the position he now found himself in. She wanted to sleep with him. He wanted to sleep with her. To think that their marriage kept them apart seemed utterly ludicrous.

Sobering, he cataloged the features that haunted him. He stroked the tip of her nose with his finger in what he hoped was an acknowledgment of her sweetness. Compared to the coarseness of his weathered hands, her skin was petal delicate.

Entreaty filled her eyes. A too-bright entreaty that went along with the flushed moistness on her cheeks and chin. She was drunk. He shouldn't take advantage of her like this.

Removing her arms from his neck, Linc pushed himself away from her and pulled back the blanket and sheets on the bed. "Get under the covers, Rachel."

"All of a sudden I'm very tired. Thank you for tucking me in, Linc."

He escaped into the bathroom to wait until she fell asleep. He wished he could leave his "problem" behind and hit the bar at the tavern again, but he didn't want to leave the room. Rachel might need him. No matter where he went or what he did, she managed to control his every move. Part of him resented it, but another part of him liked doing for Rachel. He couldn't get too used to it, though, since the days of their arrangement were slowly winding down.

He jerked open the bathroom door. Rachel lay curled on her side in the bed, her head turned away from him. She didn't move.

He tiptoed around to the empty side of the bed and checked her face. Her eyes were closed, and she was breathing heavily. Linc slipped off his boots as quietly as possible. The lady didn't have a clue she had him tied up in knots. He despised himself for thinking about her all the time, for desiring her with such vengeance he thought of little else. Such constant desire should belong to another man, the man she would eventually marry.

With a smothered oath, he lay down with his back to her and packed two pillows under his head, cursing the day he had ever laid eyes on his nemesis, Mrs. Lincoln Jefferson Monroe.

Rachel woke with a wad of cotton in her mouth, scratchy wool in her throat and the weight and sound of anvils pounding her head. Rolling onto her side, she sensed the support of a fine mattress, but the clean fragrance of the crisp sheets was her only solace. Linc was no longer there. Her cotton mouth was actually her own sour breath, and the scratch in her throat came from an undeniable thirst. Yet when she moved, the anvils pounded her head all the more, painfully real even in the shadowed darkness of the room.

She staggered from the bed, knowing death was upon her. She had never felt so twisted and achy and horrible in her life. Even if she could only whisper the words, she wanted Linc to know she still loved him. The sound of running water told her where he was. Her dying wish was enough to propel her to the half-open door of the bathroom.

With a moan of pain, she pushed on it. Sunlight from the open blinds cut into her eyes. The ringing sound of the anvil took over in her head. She leaned against the doorjamb and put her hands over her eyes. "I fear I am dying."

She opened her fingers and he appeared limned by the light and wearing only his jeans, his jaw half-covered in shaving soap. "Poor baby," he said. "Let me see."

He pried her fingers from her face. "I see what the problem is. You're green. Let me guess. You're head aches to beat the band, and the last thing you want to do is open your eyes."

"Goodness gracious," she croaked. "You must be sick with the same illness."

"Do I look sick? The truth is, I'm fine. Let's just say I've experienced the same symptoms once or twice in the past. Go back to bed. I'll be right in. I promise you'll feel better real soon."

Rachel did as she was bid, relieved that Linc was feeling well and knew what to do to save her. She carefully climbed into bed, grateful to shut her eyes against the too bright light.

She heard the sound of water running and splashing, then she saw a Linc-size shadow pass in front of her almost closed eyes. A cool washcloth was laid across her forehead. "I'll be right back," he said and disappeared from view. The door to the room clicked shut.

Eased by the coolness cutting through her pain, Rachel relaxed in the blessed quiet, secure in the knowledge that Linc always kept his word.

He reappeared several minutes later, gently announcing his presence with the soft closing of the door. "It's me, honey. Don't be scared."

Her throat was too dry to tell him she always felt protected when he was around. He entered the bathroom, and she heard water gurgle as though poured into a glass. She felt the bed sag as Linc sat down on the edge.

"Doc Monroe to the rescue. I have some aspirin for your headache."

Supporting her shoulders, he helped her sit up and removed the washcloth from her face. Pressing two aspirin into her hand, he watched while she gulped the pills and held a glass of water to her lips until she washed them down.

"I should have checked on you sooner," he murmured, taking away the glass and setting it on the nightstand. "I figured this might happen."

Wincing, Rachel sank back against the pillow. "You did?"

He wiped her face and replaced the washcloth on her forehead. "It's called a hangover. It will happen again if you drink, say, more than one little bitty beer when you go out at night."

"I think I will stick to iced tea from this day on. Ugh," she moaned and passed an arm across her eyes. "How can you stand to see me this way?"

Chuckling, Linc patted her shoulder. "Don't worry. I've seen worse in my rodeo days, believe me."

"I don't understand how," came her muffled reply from beneath her arm.

"You look great, just like you always do." Oddly, he was telling the truth. Linc smoothed her tangled hair but it defied him, spilling across the bedclothes in wild waves. No less wild was her misbuttoned blouse, bunched over her breasts, but exposing half her tummy above the waistband of her jeans. She had managed to remove her belt. It lay abandoned on the bed, alongside her bra.

"Everybody saw me make a fool of myself last night, didn't they? I'll never be able to show my face in the tavern again."

Understanding how sensitive she was to the negative judgment of others, Linc gently pulled her arm away from her eyes. "Listen to me, Rachel. You have nothing to feel ashamed of. You were simply being the person you always are: happy, lively and full of fun. Besides, what's wrong with making a fool of yourself once in a while? It's not like you have a corner on making mistakes. I've made my share, too. Everybody has. There may even be a point in life when a person decides it's okay to play the part of a fool."

Rachel grimaced as she adamantly shook her head no. Linc chuckled. "Welcome to the modern world, Rachel. Guess we could say you passed another rite of initiation."

Rachel's next rite of initiation came the next time Linc accompanied her to town. They hadn't had time on the previous trip to check out apartments, and he planned to take her grocery shopping and to a movie at the Main Street two-plex.

First they had to get out of the door of the ranch house, though.

"How many times have you told me, Linc, that I am my own person, capable of making my own decisions? This pink linen dress is perfectly fine. I've worn it to church and received many compliments on it. If it's appropriate for church, it is certainly appropriate for a Saturday night in town."

"Wear the dress, dammit, if you're so determined. You'll see what happens."

And what happened was what Rachel wanted to happen. She was the belle of the ball.

Rachel could tell Linc disapproved of her outfit by the way he stayed away, stalking his anger at the rear wall. By the time Linc rose to take his turn, she was on the floor with her fifth partner, a bottle of iced tea in her hand.

He cut in without apology. "I see you're having a good time."

She ignored his accusatory tone and answered with calm equanimity. "I'll have a better time now that you are talking to me. Shall we sit?"

"No, we're going to dance."

"I thought you didn't want to dance tonight."

"I forgot how much fun it is."

But the brooding expression on his face didn't look like he was having fun at all. While they were dancing she tried to cheer him by engaging him in conversation, and when the dance was over, she persuaded him to join the crowd she'd been sitting with. It only took a little while before she noticed that her friends at the table all seemed to be smiling at Linc as though they knew exactly what his problem was. But it was difficult for Rachel to believe that Linc was feeling jealous over her.

As he continued to drink more beer, however, his jealousy became apparent to Rachel. He wasn't paying attention to her, but when another man asked Rachel for a dance, Linc picked a fight like the ones she'd seen other men engaged in before, over some point of supposed honor. Except now it was over her.

She refrained from pointing out that Linc had encouraged the other men to dance with her, and instead had tried to herd him from the bar. But he was belligerent and would not go. Before she could insist, he was fighting not with one man, but two, creating a wild ruckus in the middle of the dance floor.

A number of the friends she and Linc had made in the past few weeks helped drag him away from the tavern and, on Rachel's direction, stuffed him into the passenger seat of the truck.

Taking the keys, she buckled him in, then climbed in on the driver's side. Linc waved away Rachel's lace-edged handkerchief and slapped a rag on the blood oozing from the cut above his eye.

"You can't drive," he accused her with sarcastic disbelief. He was put out that she had forced him to give up on that fight. He had started it and he meant to finish it even if he was beaten to a bloody pulp.

"Yes, I can," Rachel replied calmly. She started the truck to prove it. "Bud taught me."

"Bud? Bud?" Linc demanded, startled by his sense that his authority had been undermined, especially when Rachel backed the truck out of the parking lot and turned on to Main Street. "When did this happen? And where?"

"It happened in Bud's truck, since the first week I came to the ranch. We drove the back roads until I felt confident enough to brave the highway. I've got-

ten much better the last few weeks. I wished to surprise you with my strong desire to learn.''

''You've been sitting in a cab with Bud for hours
on end? Dammit, Rachel, I told you I would teach
you everything you wanted to know. He's old enough
to be your father for God's sake.''

''Nonsense. Besides, Bud is sweet on Linda.''

''Who the hell told you that?''

Rachel held on to her temper. Honestly. She
thought she had cured him of swearing. ''It's plain as
day to see, Linc. There really is no cause for you to
be jealous—''

''Jealous! I'm looking out for your welfare is all.''

Rachel blew out a sigh. ''Perhaps we should talk
this over tomorrow.''

''We're going to talk about it now.''

He wasn't picking up her signals to drop the subject. He had to be drunk. With all the fuss he was
making, she was sure of it. ''It's difficult for me to
concentrate on such a discussion while driving.''

''Pull over, then.''

''We have too long to go—''

''Pull over, I said.''

She rolled to a stop on the side of the road, determined to insist that she drive even if she had to swal-
low the keys to keep him from getting hold of them.
She took her time shifting into the parking gear in
hopes that the delay would make him realize what
folly this was.

He lunged at her and draped himself over her, in-
expertly kissing her face and pawing at the buttons
of her vest.

She grappled with him, heaving him back with all her strength. "What do you think you are doing?" She managed to elbow him in the same eye he'd been punched in.

"Ow!" He clamped his hand across his face. "That hurt!"

"It was supposed to hurt. You will behave like a gentleman, or I will kick you out of this truck and leave you by the side of the road."

He leaned back in his seat and dropped his hands in his lap, instantly contrite. "You're right," he mumbled. "I'm sorry. I don't know why I'm acting like such a jerk tonight."

"Put your seat belt back on," Rachel ordered, not quite ready to give him the full benefit of the doubt.

His broad hand was already inserting the buckle. "Yes, ma'am."

Checking the rearview mirror, Rachel put the truck in gear. "I am taking you home now."

"Good idea," he said. "I really am sorry, Rachel."

"I have never seen you act this way. What has come over you?"

He clenched his fists, thinking about her dancing with other men. Repulsed by his inability to control himself and worse, proving it with fits of jealousy, he leaned back against the headrest and closed his eyes. "Forget it, will you?"

"I will not forget it. What I will do is drive you home."

She shifted the truck into gear and smoothly pulled out onto the road.

He brooded for the rest of the two-hour trip.

When they arrived home, he allowed her to minister to him, accepting the cold compress she placed on his cheekbone. Helping him up the stairs to bed, he even allowed her to enter the territory of his room. She took off his torn and bloodied shirt and told him to lie down. Groaning, he lay on the bed and she pulled off his boots.

"Stay," he said, clasping her wrist.

It was at that moment that Rachel felt very aware that they were together on the bed. The fact that he had his jeans on eased her mind somewhat, and she also reminded herself that he was obviously sorely injured. But she also recalled that his injury had not stopped his aggressive action toward her in the truck.

"I will make you comfortable before I retire for the night."

"I like the way you phrase things. Like 'retire for the night.' Sounds like a century-old character from a book."

"In The Community all the books were written at least a century ago. It is how they maintain a tie to the past."

"Did you hear what you said? You said 'they,' not 'we.' That means you have left The Community behind you."

"Is that good?"

"Very good," he said with a wry half smile. "I can't believe you learned how to drive. Do you like it?"

"I do like to go fast."

"How fast?"

"Fast enough that Bud mentioned the penalties for

speeding tickets. But the wind was whistling and the engine of the truck made me want to press down harder on the accelerator. I felt as if I would take off and fly.''

Linc snapped his fingers. ''That's another thing I need to do—take you on a plane ride.''

''All these rides,'' she teased. ''What's next—a deer on the run?''

''How about an elk? I rode one once.''

''You didn't.''

''Sure did.'' He spread his hand across his chest in pride. ''Got in trouble with the law for it, too. But I'd won the all-around rodeo title two years in a row. At that point I was foolish enough to think that challenging myself with the prospect of riding a real wild animal was a good idea.''

Rachel injected some healthy skepticism in her voice. ''How did you catch this elk?''

''With my bare hands.''

''Liar,'' she chided.

''I roped him. What did you expect? I had two of my buddies hold the rope while I mounted the son of a gun. He was some ride.''

''I wish I could have seen it.''

''I bet you could have ridden him yourself.''

His compliment created a sense of tenderness in her, a sense that he had treated her with tenderness many times, which she had refused sometimes to see. Simply bidding for her had been a tender act. And bringing her here. And giving her Summer to train.

And being willing to teach her so very much.

It came upon her how much she loved him. It had little to do with her longing that they be well and truly married. In his world, sharing a bed hardly constituted reason to marry. There had to be strong feelings behind the bond to justify it, and she didn't mean feelings of a practical nature having to do with convenience. In his world, marriage meant more. The bond came from mutual want and not need. And that's where the purest and most nurturing love came from.

Rachel thought of her horses, thought of how her methods depended on her allowing the horse to want to come to her when he was ready rather than the other way around. If she forced the horse into a corner or chased him, even from afar, he would run or he would fight. But never would he stay. Unless his spirit had been broken.

She had no right to pull Linc along with her, to press this claim that he honor vows he had been forced to make. This was the truth he wanted her to grasp. It was what he'd been trying to teach her all along.

Love and understanding like this was such a gift, she thought, for both of them, whether he acknowledged it or not. Leaving the ranch, leaving Linc, did not mean she had failed. And if she did choose to lie with him again, love rather than duty would inspire her. Progress, she thought. Progress. Sometimes it came like that of a tiny ant, scaling one tall grass blade at a time.

Nine

"**L**inc?"

Rachel's voice. He groaned at the hopeful beating of his heart. He'd spent the last twenty-four hours berating himself for acting like a lovesick fool in front of Rachel and he still wasn't cured. It was two o'clock in the morning. Bad enough that he was up and awake. He opened the door.

"I was worried," she said. "I saw your light was on."

"I'm having trouble sleeping, that's all. Go back to bed."

She leaned against the doorway, wearing a long, white nightgown. Because the glow from the hall light behind her spilled into the room, her shadow did too, playing with his feet. He'd been pacing the floor. "Why can't you sleep?" she asked.

Because I think about you all the time. Because I miss you. Because I hurt you and I'm sorry. Because I want to make love to you again. "I have too much on my mind."

She stepped barefoot inside his room. "A good rubdown is what you need. Lay down, please."

"You need your sleep. Go back to bed. I'm fine."

"You've done such nice things for me. I'd like to do something nice for you."

"Tell me why you are still awake then?" he asked, plumping his pillows as though he planned to stretch out the moment she was gone. "Morning will be here before you know it."

"Linc, this may not be the right time to ask you this, but what else do I need to learn before I'm ready to move to town?"

"You're right, Rachel. This isn't the time. I'm tired and you need your rest. We'll talk about it at supper, okay?"

"It's been very much on my mind lately. I promised to do my best to learn all I could from you, Linc. I wonder if the time has come for me to leave."

"It's not," he said curtly.

"Need I try harder?"

"No, Rachel," he replied, sighing. "Nobody has learned faster or worked harder than you. Remember, though, I made promises, too. We haven't found an apartment for you yet. Or a job. And I promised to take you on an airplane and show you what it feels like to fly."

"I already know what it feels like. I've done it ever since you brought me to this ranch."

"What's this all about, Rachel? If I didn't know better, I'd say you want to move to town."

"You've taught me well, Linc. From now on, I'll take good care of myself."

"Don't be silly. Where will you live?"

She pulled out the local newspaper and showed him the classified ad section. "I made several telephone calls, comparing rents and accommodations. I've decided on this furnished room. It's reasonably priced and within walking distance of Main Street."

Linc scanned the newspaper through his haze of disbelief. "Linda must have helped you."

"No, she went to visit her sister in Helena, remember?"

"Bud, then."

"I did it myself, Linc."

Linc tossed the newspaper aside. "You still have to find a job."

"The manager at the tavern hired me on as a waitress. I'm working the day shift. The salary is enough to pay my basic necessities. Tips should cover the rest of my expenses."

"Tips? You're depending on tips to support you?" Floored by how much she'd done on her own, Linc jumped on the smallest detail. "I thought I taught you better than that."

She shrugged. "You taught me very well. If the job doesn't pay enough, then I will get another one."

"What about Summer?" he retorted, infuriated by her immediate answer to every one of his questions. She must have been planning this for some time.

"The horse needs you. What are you going to do about her?"

"I hoped I could continue to train her here. May I?"

At last she'd said something that made sense. If Summer remained her project, then Rachel would have to come back to care for her. "I wouldn't have it any other way. Look, Rachel, I'd be remiss if I didn't tell you again that your talent is wasted on the tavern. You should be looking for a job where you'd be working with horses, and you know it."

"Eventually, I'll end up on a ranch similar to this one, doing what I do best. For the time being, however, I think it would be good for me to experience town life, as you recommended."

It took effort to control the ire he felt at hearing his so-called recommendations spouted back at him. She must have some other reason for wanting to move. Maybe she was interested in some greenhorn townie.

Except he had been down this road with Rachel before. Jealousy was the stupidest card he ever played with her. He refused to make the same mistake again. She attracted male attention, sure, for obvious reasons. Pretty, lively, and smarter than a whip, she was also the most loyal person he had ever known. "You think town life would do you good?" he asked, listening carefully to the answer.

"Yes, Linc. I'd like to move on Monday if it's all right with you. It will give me a few days to pack my things. Plus, I'd like to go to the local church one last time and say my goodbyes."

"Sure," he said roughly, pushing aside the prospect of goodbye in favor of the much better prospect of having his life back again. Hell, he could go wild if he wanted, just like the old days when he was a young buck on the circuit, free to do whatever he pleased.

He didn't remember feeling hollow at the prospect, however.

He turned his back on her and went to the window, staring out into space. He was having a hard time breathing. He was also having a hard time keeping himself from lashing out at her. Though she hadn't stated the exact time of day yet, she was going to leave. That was that. He should be happy for her. "I want you to have Summer," he said.

"You don't have to do that, Linc."

"Yes, I do!" He stayed at the window, hating himself for revealing that much emotion to her. With monumental effort, he worked to get his voice under control. "Summer means the world to you."

Rachel didn't know what to say, not to the truth. But this wasn't how she wanted to leave him. And she wanted a vehicle to return to the ranch to see Linda, Bud...and most of all, Linc. How could she tell him? What words could possibly describe what he meant to her? Then it dawned on her. She didn't need words.

Rachel crept closer to Linc's bare back after he'd turned on his side, away from her. She placed her fingertips on him and felt his muscles tense. Skin covered them, firm skin. Yet he seemed to tremble under her fingertips.

"Go back to your room, Rachel. I'm fine now."

"You do not want me to do this?"

Using both hands, she stroked his back, making the strength of her presence known. He carried such a weight on his shoulders. She sought to relieve it, if only for this moment. Except she didn't want this moment to end.

He stiffened when she kissed the curve of his spine between his shoulder blades. "How many times do I have to tell you, Rachel? This is wrong. I won't let it happen again."

But he didn't turn around to push her away. Gathering her courage, she kissed him again. Her fingers grazed his skin with the same pressure as her lips. Traveling the width of his shoulders, she traced ridges and valleys of increasing tension. But it was not the tension of dislike. The atmosphere in the room had changed. She could feel the difference, feel how he withheld himself from her with only limited success.

If she spoke, she would shatter the illusion that he was the one in control. So she let her hands do the talking, massaging him deeply, as though soothing his muscles was her only intent. But her own body was changing. The now-familiar fluttering of her heart was spreading, making her feel shivery all over like a newborn colt. She felt an overwhelming desire to wrap her arms around him. But her instincts told her it was too early for that.

Instead she concentrated on the line of his spine and pressed her thumbs on either side, working her way up to the top where his hair brushed the back of his neck. He grunted an assent and, emboldened, she buried her fingers in his hair.

Linc felt the threat of what she offered him. The only way he could protect himself from any future offerings was to make her hate him. Hate him as he hated himself for taking her away from the safest and most familiar haven there was for someone as innocent and naive as she. He wanted her to hate him so she'd walk out the door without a backward glance. What better way than to take this terrible, unsolicited trust she gave him?

He turned around to face her and brushed his mouth against her forehead, torturing himself with the milky taste of her skin. She trembled, and he felt the inevitable hunger he had for her coursing through his body. He knew he shouldn't be doing this.

His hand pressed until she tilted her face up, obeying his wordless direction. He kissed her mouth, the lips alone, rubbing them into swollen sensitivity. She returned what was on his mind. The tip of her tongue touched his lips, rimming them. He swallowed thickly and held himself back as punishment for letting her give anything at all to him. He was the teacher. He was the one who should be giving to her. "You always have the right to say no," he whispered. "Say it, Rachel, and I'll stop."

"I don't want you to stop."

Both hands cradled her head, forcing it back enough for her to see his determination and hear the command in his voice. "Say the word *no,* Rachel."

"I don't want you to stop."

She never did what he wanted her to do. And now

he was glad. Far too glad. He kissed her again, drizzling warmth over her mouth, going slowly, slowly enough to cause him to throb with utter desire. He couldn't wait. She was willing. Yet there was so much more at stake here.

He thumbed the hollows that carved her cheeks. "You always have the right to say no," he whispered. "Say no to me, Rachel. Tell me to stop."

"Is this another lesson?"

For him it was. He gazed into her slumberous eyes. Reflected back was the tattered remnants of innocence, tattered like his conscience and the nerves scraping his spine. "What if I was the one who said no?" he asked. "Would you stop?"

"Yes." The tip of her tongue trailed kisses from his chin to his cheek, back to his jaw. "Do you want me to stop?"

He closed his eyes, feeling his throat thicken. He was the student. Not her.

The throbbing in his groin matched the throbbing of his heart, constricting his chest and the muscles of his arms that wanted to hold on to her. He wanted to keep her safe. He wanted her near in order to protect her from harm. "Yes, it's another lesson. Don't let the passion of the moment overwhelm your judgment."

Now was the time he should push her away. Her whispered confessions were gifts, gifts he didn't deserve. From the beginning.

He lifted her into a sitting position alongside him. Hair mussed and lips swollen from kissing, Rachel cocked her head as if ready for his touch, for anything his heart desired. The way he wanted her actually hurt, churning his insides and constricting his chest—shredded by this constant hunger for what he would not allow himself to have. "Rachel," he whispered. "I'm glad you came to be with me, at least for a while."

She pressed herself into his arms. He turned toward her like a panther might, and he pounced, devouring her, demanding everything she sought to give.

She gripped his shoulders, all too aware of the power she had unleashed, the power of a man held too tightly in check. There was danger in such power; however, there was glory in it, too. And she did glory in it, tasting him fully—meeting his urgency with all of her own.

She had to rid herself of her clothes. Then the aching would cease. He must have felt the same urgency, for he stood and peeled off his clothes at the same moment she did.

Naked, he swept her naked off her feet and whirled her around like some fool gone out of his head. He was a fool because she started to laugh and he laughed, too, whirling and whirling until he was dizzy with her, choked up and breathless with her. He kissed her again, only tenderly, letting her breathe. His tongue touched her lips, tracing both with deliberation, edging his teeth on her lower lip and finally biting it with gentleness.

His whole body ached. He brushed her forehead over and over again with his lips, and wisps of her hair whisked his face, stirring him to weave his fingers to the warmth of her scalp. He strung kisses along the high bones of her cheeks. Easing her down the front of his rigid body, he experienced the sweetest pain he'd ever felt. "Rachel," he said in a voice made hoarse by desire. "Help me. Help me, if you want me to stop."

"Green light is go. I don't want stops. I just want you."

"You've got me." He caught her up and held her tight, recalling what would happen when he did, tripling his ache. Except the feeling went further than that. It spiked his blood, speared his skin. His hands shook with it. Afraid he might scare her, he loosened his hold and gazed into the depths of her eyes. Crystalline blue, they blazed with the hot sunshine of natural, pure desire.

He pulled her to the bed and pulled her down on top of him. She giggled. He kissed her into seriousness, into letting her body melt and pillowing her breasts against his chest. He lifted her hips, guiding her to straddle his stomach. She sat up and tossed her head, revealing breasts that budded at their centers when he caressed them.

His sex throbbed, searching for home. She reached behind her and closed her hand around him. Linc nearly lost it right there. He lifted his head and suckled her. She moaned and squirmed to give him more of her, and he obliged, supporting her weight in his lap.

Pleasuring her became its own reward. He found pulse points and kissed them. His tongue dwelled in the hollows formed by her collarbone and shoulder. He shifted her from his lap to the bed, turning her so she was lying on her stomach. Broad hands soothed the tension in her muscles, laying her out on the bed like a rag doll. He paid special attention to the round-ness of her hips and nipped her gently on her rear. Giggling, she twisted to look at him, and he used her momentum to flip her onto her back.

Keeping his gaze trained on her face, he kissed the inside of her thigh. Her teeth snagged her lower lip as he worked his way up, and her chest rose and fell with the effort it took to breathe. "Don't stop," she said. "Please don't stop."

She had already reached dewpoint. Guided by her ragged drags of air, he gave her more moisture and felt her throbbing response beckoning for him. She grasped his arms and forced him to meet her face-to-face and heart-to-heart.

Silken strength opened beneath him. Poised at her entrance, he found the remnants of control and slowed. But she didn't want him to slow down. She thrust her hips upward, sheathing him suddenly and completely. The slickness alone was enough to drive him to the brink, never mind how tight she was.

Driven to the brink herself, she pulsed around him. All he had to do was guide her movements for a few moments, then the liquid rush began. He aimed there, seeing how ecstasy made her soar, and he soared him-self, holding her in a mutually trembling embrace.

He hadn't planned the day to end like this, he thought awhile later. He hadn't planned her stay to end like this, either. And now he didn't want it to end. To have her in his bed, to hold her close and feel how she pierced the darkness for him, giving him insights he hadn't experienced before was precious.

Shafts of moonlight bathed her in varying shades of luminous silver and gray. Not wanting to disturb her, he gently placed his hand on her rounded hip and watched her sleep. He wished he had listened to her sooner. Or better yet, listened to what his gut had been telling him all along. Instead, he'd been too damned determined on forcing his version of freedom on her.

Tenderly he rubbed her, putting aside his desire to immediately make love to her again. They had plenty of time for that. A lifetime. And she needed her sleep. He, on the other hand, had enough energy for both of them.

He rolled off the bed and stretched. Reveling in the ordinary, he showered and shaved and leisurely pulled on his clothes. All he could think about was showering her with gifts that symbolized his love for her, for he realized finally that was what he felt. He'd give her a wedding band that matched the filigree on her engagement ring. And a truck of her own. She deserved those things and more. He wanted to give her roses—the white bridal roses she should have had at their wedding. He wanted to weave daisies in her hair and find Texas bluebells to match her eyes. He wanted to make her laugh by showering her with blooms, sharing the sense of freedom they created together. She inspired such devotion in him, such an appreciation for life.

Before she'd come along, he'd been going through the motions, pretending he didn't notice the dismaying lack of satisfaction he felt for finally attaining the success he'd always thought he wanted. Rachel didn't have the ability to pretend. She didn't allow anyone around her to pretend, either. She had lifted the clouds from his eyes.

But giving her independence meant giving her up. He wasn't sure he could do that. The thought alone was enough to give him another serious case of the shakes. Once she tasted freedom, she might decide the love she claimed to feel wasn't really love at all. If that happened, his life wouldn't mean much anymore. What was the point of building his business if Rachel wasn't there to share it with him?

Thanks to her, he'd learned his purpose in life. It had nothing to do with horses, rodeoing or ranching, either.

He went downstairs and looked out the window. He squinted into the sky and scanned the mountains, which had heaved up high above the prairies so long ago. The loneliness of the land hit him as never before. But it didn't have to be lonely, as long as he had Rachel by his side.

He made breakfast for them both, placed both meals on a tray and went up the stairs to surprise her in bed.

Except she was no longer there.

After spending the rest of the morning searching for her, it dawned on Linc to check Summer's stall. Empty. Linc realized that Rachel was well and truly gone. He swept his cowboy hat from his head and balanced the brim between his hands, standing with his head bowed in that century-old gesture of humility.

He didn't have to wonder why she left. Their time had run out. Last night he had even continued to make his unwillingness to love her all too clear. He'd never even gotten around to saying the words to her. The words she had said that had meant so much to him.

I love you.

Even *he* didn't believe he deserved a second chance. He'd pushed her away for too long.

He wanted to give her children. Children with turquoise eyes and dreamers' hearts. He wanted to teach them to be free like their mother was, free in spirit, indulging in the bliss that came with the simplest of goodness-gracious delights.

Before Rachel his life had been empty. Though he had sensed the emptiness, he'd refused to understand what was behind it. He'd hidden behind his work. He'd pretended building his ranch and clientele were challenge enough for a man in this life.

At the end, what did that kind of stuff mean? Yes, he would feel the satisfaction of doing his job well, but when it came time for him to stand in front of Heaven's pearly gates, his work would be nothing but memories. His whole life was built on memories. There was nothing tangible. What lives had he touched? Had he made a difference in any of them? Or had he stayed mostly to himself, refusing offers of help, pretending that he didn't mind how alone he was?

Horse trainers were a dime a dozen. When push

came to shove, he wouldn't have a problem giving it all up for the woman he truly loved.

Rachel saw the first rose from her height on Summer's back. The white rose lay alone on the trail, behind the boarding stables nearest to town. An ivory pebble in the dust, its petals glistened with dew. The green of the leaves glistened, too, intense as emeralds. Intense as the searching look of a lone hunter, sitting on the back of his favorite mount, the Paint. Linc's eyes narrowed when she spotted him. He slipped off his horse's back and stood with the horse in the middle of the trail, blocking Rachel's path.

"Hello," he said.

At the husky sound of his low, soft voice, Rachel felt a stinging pain stab her heart. She had missed him terribly. For two weeks now, every cell in her body had yearned to go back to him, without conditions or reservations. She was a modern woman of the world now, free to do as she pleased. As long as she was acting out of genuine love for him, what difference did it make whether or not he loved her? As Linc once said, there was nothing wrong with somebody *choosing* to act like a fool.

Seemingly of its own volition, her spine stiffened. She nodded to acknowledge him. "Lincoln," she said.

"I thought I might find you on one of these trails. When I first started looking to buy land in Montana, I loaded up my trailer and started driving from town to town. Tall Timbers was the first place I liked enough to spend any time at. I rode some of these trails. The view from here of the mountains, of the valley, convinced me that I wanted to settle around here.''

For Lincoln Monroe, that was a veritable speech. There didn't seem to be a point to it, however. ''What do you want?''

''It's very simple, Rachel. I want you. I love you.''

Time stood still. The impulse to turn around and retreat dissipated under his careful watch of her every move. He was waiting for her to run, ready to give chase as any male animal would. Her only option was to face him in the same way he faced her—as equals. That was why she hadn't gone back to him, crawling back to him. There *was* a difference between choosing to play the part of a fool and *being* a fool. Linc was the one who taught her how to distinguish the former from the latter. Rather than try to get by him, she turned her horse around. ''I'm sorry, but you can't have me, Linc,'' she said over her shoulder.

A lariat snaked in a sudden circle above her head. Then she was caught around the shoulders with only enough slack to let her stay in the saddle. Linc whipped by on his horse and caught Summer by her bridle. ''Whoa, there,'' he said. ''I didn't hear you say you don't love me.''

''Let me go this instant.''

''I have an apology to make first,'' he said, and jumped off his horse and knelt in the dust. ''It's the kind of apology that I'm supposed to be on bended knee for.''

''Lincoln Monroe, what are you doing?''

"It occurred to me—I never officially asked you to marry me."

Her horse shifted from foot to foot nervously, spurred to such movement, Rachel was sure, by the sudden and terrible trembling of her rider. "You bought me, remember?"

"You, Rachel, can't be bought. Not in body and certainly not in soul. Don't you understand? We were meant to be together."

"You're not to be trusted. You told me that."

"You're right. I can't change the past. You can find solace in the wide-open spaces. I should know. But I also know that a love such as ours is as precious as life, that it cannot and should not be wasted."

"Nonsense. Go back to your ranch. It needs you more than I do."

"You may be interested to know that Bud is taking care of the ranch. I'm thinking of selling."

Shocked, she swallowed hard. "That ranch is your dream. You will do no such thing."

"Who's going to stop me?"

"You ask too much of me, Linc."

"No, Rachel. The truth is I haven't asked enough. But I'm asking now. I'm asking for a second chance. I'm asking you to forgive me. I should have told you I loved you long before now." He swept off his hat and placed it over his heart, having eyes for only her. "I'm asking, Rachel. Will you be my wife?"

Was he making fun of her? Rachel hated to think it, but he was acting so differently, she concluded it might be so. "As you may recall, I already was your wife. It didn't work out." Rachel pushed up the slackening lariat past her shoulders and threw it on the ground. "Goodbye, Linc."

Instinct told her to move past him without a backward glance. Her mind, however, said that he was a man with considerable pride—pride she was about to walk over. But she had pride, too. And she had always trusted her instincts. They had never let her down before.

She steered by him. Linc still knelt on the ground with his hat in his hand, watching her intensely all the while. "I'm not giving up," he called to her retreating back.

Distracted by the events of that morning, Rachel had to scold herself into paying attention when she went to the tavern where she now worked. Her boss had informed her that a new bartender had been hired on, and though she was a new employee herself, she was expected to show him the ropes.

Show him the ropes. When she heard the old and memorable figure of speech, she couldn't help but shake her head. "At least I know what the ropes are, thanks to Linc."

Then, crazily enough, she heard Linc's voice greet the tavern owner by name. At least, she thought it was Linc's voice. Of course she had to be mistaken. She turned around and realized she hadn't been.

"Rachel," said her boss, the tavern owner. "Meet our new bartender, Lincoln Monroe."

"Howdy, Rachel. I'm happy to see you."

"I'm sorry," she said on a burst of disbelief, "but I know this man and I refuse to work with him."

"Is that so?" queried the tavern owner. "It sounds like the two of you have a few things to talk about. If you can't resolve them by the time your shift ends at midnight, don't bother coming back to work tomorrow."

The moment the owner left for the night, Rachel rushed to speak to Linc. "Don't do this to me, please. I-I'm content here."

"You deserve more than contentment. You deserve a wild and crazy man who loves you, who'll push you to be wild and crazy and foolish, too. We belong together, Rachel. You may as well give in, because you're not getting rid of me. I'll hang around until I really do drive you crazy."

Rachel folded her arms and tipped her chin in defiance. "Stop this. You are a rancher. You have a ranch to run."

"Bud and Linda can run it. You were right about them, Rachel. They make a great team. They've decided to get married, in fact. But the bottom line for me is, the ranch doesn't mean much without having you around to share it. I'll marry you in a church, in the courthouse, in the fields, I don't care, as long as you're my wife."

She dashed tears from her eyes. "For the last time—I was your wife. I enjoyed it while it lasted. However, it's over now."

"It's not over, not as long as I love you and you love me. And I do love you, Rachel. You always made me *want* to say it. I was just too bullheaded to step down from my high horse and admit that I didn't have the power to set you free. You were already free—free in spirit. I was the one who wasn't free to be the man I should have been to you. Let me be your husband, Rachel. A real husband. One who wants to share his life and all his love with you."

He opened his arms. Rachel didn't even hesitate. For the first time in her twenty-eight years, she felt utterly loved and understood. She flew to him, and he hugged her and spun her around, the wild beating of his heart entwining with the wild beat of hers. Together they laughed, and Rachel squeezed her eyes shut, buoyed by such high hopes, her old fears were swept away.

At least for the moment.

Ten

Standing on the cool tile floor of her bathroom, Rachel shivered and slipped on her nightclothes with much trepidation, as nervous on this, her second wedding night, as she had been on her first. Though she was well acquainted with her husband, the thought of the lovemaking soon to come had shifted her imagination into overdrive.

Of course Linc would be gentle with her. Of course he would understand her trepidations and fears. Linc had always listened to her, and even if he didn't agree, the resolution they arrived at inevitably moved them forward to new discoveries about their inward selves. It was one of the things she most loved about him. He'd helped her see how resourceful she truly was.

Yet the image that stared back at her in the mirror did not reflect her image of a resourceful wife. She'd kept her hair loose and free because she so enjoyed the pleasure Linc took from touching it. Yet the newly shining and sweet-smelling waves that teased her shoulders and the sides of her face made her appear far more girlish than she wanted to convey. Coupled with the high neck and prim yoke of the fine lawn nightgown her mother had sewn so many years ago, Rachel just *knew* Linc would think that her aim in wearing such an old-fashioned outfit was to remind him how foolish and inexperienced she truly was.

According to the advice of Linda and Mary Lou, Rachel had taken to wearing T-shirts to bed. Going to her chiffarobe, she inspected her various T-shirts. All were emblazoned with some kind of funny saying or logo and barely covered her midriff. To meet Linc wearing a brightly colored T-shirt and her underwear offended her sense of propriety. Forward thinking and modern as she had become, she believed that love-making was special, especially when it was planned and anticipated. Such an occasion demanded the appropriate dress. The virginal nightgown would have to do.

She opened the bathroom door and saw golden candlelight flickering upon their bedroom wall. Linc was already there, she sensed, waiting for her.

The leap of her blood in excited anticipation contrasted sharply with the slowing of her steps. How foolish would he think her when she appeared looking like some sort of untouched angel from the heavenly realm?

She paused in front of the bed; aware of the damp-
ness of her hands—especially her right hand, which
clutched the fabric of her nightgown far too tightly.
If she were truly brave and resourceful, she would
shed the gown. She would climb into the bed naked.
Yet Rachel couldn't forget her memory of her mother
lovingly stitching the gown, describing the use of it
for her wedding night and how the man she would
marry would know to go slowly with her when he
saw it. And Rachel knew more than anything else that
that was exactly the reaction from Linc she needed.

Holding her breath, she crept into bed, her hand
touching the lace at her throat. Her attention was immediately drawn to the fact that under the covers,
Linc was in jeans. His black hat was tipped forward
over his eyes, covering most of his face, as well.

To think that she'd been worrying all this time,
when Linc was in actuality fast asleep, had Rachel
covering her mouth in something close to giddy relief.
All she had to do was lie here beside him. When he
awoke, the rest would take care of itself. If she
wanted, she could even blow out the candles to put
the room in darkness. Then there would be only feelings and the touches that turned those feelings into
action.

"Come here," he said.

Her ears were deceiving her. There was no indication that he had spoken—he lay absolutely motionless on the bed in the same position as before.

"Rachel," he chided, entirely relaxed except for
the slight movement of his jaw. "Come here."

Her body obeyed even though her heart remained

unsure. This was not how she thought he would be tonight, even in most satisfying imaginings. It was almost as if he didn't care what she looked like or how she wished to present herself. Certainly he didn't care how he presented himself to her.

When she halted at his side of the bed, his hand snaked out to stroke her hip. "You look beautiful. Perfect in every way."

"How would you know? You can't see me."

He tilted his hat back enough for her to see his partly closed eyes, narrowed eyes that glinted in awareness of her. "Do you really think I would miss a moment of your coming to me? I got here an hour ago. I wanted to make sure everything was clean and pretty for you. I thought about taking off my clothes and getting under the covers, but that seemed like I was rushing things. And tonight I definitely don't want to rush." He sent her a half grin alight with mischief. "Unless rushing is what you want."

She knelt on the floor and took the hand that had settled so lovingly on her hip, quieting some of her fears. But not all of them. "What if I said I don't want to do anything at all?"

He squeezed the fingers entwined tightly with his. "I'd say you were frightened. I'd say I have never let that stop me before. That's because I sensed from the moment I met you that you didn't want fears to stop you, either. Tell me what they are and, whether it takes days or years, we'll face them all down together."

She bent her head in prayer. Watching her, Linc prayed, too, prayed that she could find it in her heart to trust him with her secret fears and dreams in the same way he trusted her with his. "I fear my mother would disapprove of my wearing of this nightdress. She made it as part of my trousseau, as the gown I was to wear on my wedding night. Yet, try as I might, I know in my heart that tonight is not really our wedding night. I know it is silly but I feel I am dishonoring her somehow."

Linc fingered her collar, smoothing the lace at her throat. "Rachel, you did wear this nightgown on our 'real' wedding night. I saw you in it. I remember it well."

"How? We never, we never—"

"Just because we didn't sleep together that night doesn't mean I didn't spend the night in your room. I watched you sleep. I even touched you. Here," he said, stroking her forehead. "I couldn't stop myself. I wanted to make love to you."

"Then why didn't you wake me?"

"I didn't understand why then, but looking back now, I know the time wasn't right. You see, I'm afraid of how you'll react sometimes, too."

"You are?"

"I am. Just like you. Will you help me get over it?"

"Yes, Linc. What can I do?"

"Tell me you love me."

"I love you."

"And I love you. It feels good to hear, doesn't it? I love you, Rachel. I love everything about you, from the courage you showed just now in confessing what's going on inside that head of yours, to the clothes you wear…or don't wear,'' he added, and winked.

Rachel winked in return, surging with an emotion she had never fully felt before. Love flowed like sunshine through her body. She rose from her knees. Linc straightened to meet her, throwing his legs over the side of the bed and guiding her to sit on his lap.

Wreathed by his arms, Rachel snuggled against him, smelling the spicy, sage scent of his skin. The power of his love permeated her, and as it did, her body came alive. She pulsed with it, with senses looking for fulfillment and the roller-coaster ride he took her on when they reached unadulterated awe. There were no more doubts. No more enumerations of the mistakes she might make or recriminations about the past.

What lived in her now was acceptance, an acceptance that encompassed everything she was and everything she wanted to be. Linc was her love, her guide to her very soul—as she was to his. Together they would ride against the winds of change and the challenges of life. Forever.

* * * * *

SILHOUETTE'S 20ᵀᴴ ANNIVERSARY CONTEST
OFFICIAL RULES
NO PURCHASE NECESSARY TO ENTER

1. To enter, follow directions published in the offer to which you are responding. Contest begins 1/1/00 and ends on 8/24/00 (the "Promotion Period"). Method of entry may vary. Mailed entries must be postmarked by 8/24/00, and received by 8/31/00.

2. During the Promotion Period, the Contest may be presented via the Internet. Entry via the Internet may be restricted to residents of certain geographic areas that are disclosed on the Web site. To enter via the Internet, if you are a resident of a geographic area in which Internet entry is permissible, follow the directions displayed on-line, including typing your essay of 100 words or fewer telling us "Where In The World Your Love Will Come Alive." On-line entries must be received by 11:59 p.m. Eastern Standard time on 8/24/00. Limit one e-mail entry per person, household and e-mail address per day, per presentation. If you are a resident of a geographic area in which entry via the Internet is permissible, you may, in lieu of submitting an entry on-line, enter by mail, by hand-printing your name, address, telephone number and contest number/name on an 8"x 11" plain piece of paper and telling us in 100 words or fewer "Where In The World Your Love Will Come Alive," and mailing via first-class mail to: Silhouette 20ᵗʰ Anniversary Contest, (in the U.S.) P.O. Box 9069, Buffalo, NY 14269-9069; (In Canada) P.O. Box 637, Fort Erie, Ontario, Canada L2A 5X3. Limit one 8"x 11" mailed entry per person, household and e-mail address per day. On-line and/or 8"x 11" mailed entries received from persons residing in geographic areas in which Internet entry is not permissible will be disqualified. No liability is assumed for lost, late, incomplete, inaccurate, nondelivered or misdirected mail, or misdirected e-mail, for technical, hardware or software failures of any kind, lost or unavailable network connection, or failed, incomplete, garbled or delayed computer transmission or any human error which may occur in the receipt or processing of the entries in the contest.

3. Essays will be judged by a panel of members of the Silhouette editorial and marketing staff based on the following criteria:

   > Sincerity (believability, credibility)—50%
   >
   > Originality (freshness, creativity)—30%
   >
   > Aptness (appropriateness to contest ideas)—20%

   Purchase or acceptance of a product offer does not improve your chances of winning. In the event of a tie, duplicate prizes will be awarded.

4. All entries become the property of Harlequin Enterprises Ltd., and will not be returned. Winner will be determined no later than 10/31/00 and will be notified by mail. Grand Prize winner will be required to sign and return Affidavit of Eligibility within 15 days of receipt of notification. Noncompliance within the time period may result in disqualification and an alternative winner may be selected. All municipal, provincial, federal, state and local laws and regulations apply. Contest open only to residents of the U.S. and Canada who are 18 years of age or older, and is void wherever prohibited by law. Internet entry is restricted solely to residents of those geographical areas in which Internet entry is permissible. Employees of Torstar Corp., their affiliates, agents and members of their immediate families are not eligible. Taxes on the prizes are the sole responsibility of winners. Entry and acceptance of any prize offered constitutes permission to use winner's name, photograph or other likeness for the purposes of advertising, trade and promotion on behalf of Torstar Corp. without further compensation to the winner, unless prohibited by law. Torstar Corp and D.L. Blair, Inc., their parents, affiliates and subsidiaries, are not responsible for errors in printing or electronic presentation of contest or entries. In the event of printing or other errors which may result in unintended prize values or duplication of prizes, all affected contest materials or entries shall be null and void. If for any reason the Internet portion of the contest is not capable of running as planned, including infection by computer virus, bugs, tampering, unauthorized intervention, fraud, technical failures, or any other causes beyond the control of Torstar Corp. which corrupt or affect the administration, secrecy, fairness, integrity or proper conduct of the contest, Torstar Corp. reserves the right, at its sole discretion, to disqualify any individual who tampers with the entry process and to cancel, terminate, modify or suspend the contest or the Internet portion thereof. In the event of a dispute regarding an on-line entry, the entry will be deemed submitted by the authorized holder of the e-mail account submitted at the time of entry. Authorized account holder is defined as the natural person who is assigned to an e-mail address by an Internet access provider, on-line service provider or other organization that is responsible for arranging e-mail address for the domain associated with the submitted e-mail address.

5. Prizes: Grand Prize—a $10,000 vacation to anywhere in the world. Travelers (at least one must be 18 years of age or older) or parent or guardian if one traveler is a minor, must sign and return a Release of Liability prior to departure. Travel must be completed by December 31, 2001, and is subject to space and accommodations availability. Two hundred (200) Second Prizes—a two-book limited edition autographed collector set from one of the Silhouette Anniversary authors: Nora Roberts, Diana Palmer, Linda Howard or Annette Broadrick (value $10.00 each set). All prizes are valued in U.S. dollars.

6. For a list of winners (available after 10/31/00), send a self-addressed, stamped envelope to: Harlequin Silhouette 20ᵗʰ Anniversary Winners, P.O. Box 4200, Blair, NE 68009-4200.

Contest sponsored by Torstar Corp., P.O. Box 9042, Buffalo, NY 14269-9042.

ENTER FOR
A CHANCE TO WIN*

Silhouette's 20ᵗʰ Anniversary Contest

Tell Us Where in the World
You Would Like *Your* Love To Come Alive...
And We'll Send the Lucky Winner There!

Silhouette wants to take you wherever
your happy ending can come true.

Here's how to enter: Tell us, in 100 words or less,
where you want to go to make your love come alive!

In addition to the grand prize, there will be 200
runner-up prizes, collector's-edition book sets
autographed by one of the Silhouette anniversary
authors: **Nora Roberts, Diana Palmer,
Linda Howard** or **Annette Broadrick**.

DON'T MISS YOUR CHANCE TO WIN!
ENTER NOW! No Purchase Necessary

Silhouette®
Where love comes alive™

Name: _____

Address: _____

City: _____ State/Province: _____

Zip/Postal Code: _____

Mail to Harlequin Books: **In the U.S.**: P.O. Box 9069, Buffalo, NY
14269-9069; **In Canada**: P.O. Box 637, Fort Erie, Ontario, L4A 5X3

*No purchase necessary—for contest details send a self-addressed stamped envelope to:
Silhouette's 20ᵗʰ Anniversary Contest, P.O. Box 9069, Buffalo, NY, 14269-9069 (include
contest name on self-addressed envelope). Residents of Washington and Vermont may
omit postage. Open to Cdn. (excluding Quebec) and U.S. residents who are 18 or over.
Void where prohibited. Contest ends August 31, 2000.

PS20CON_R